# HAIL TO THE KING

# HAIL TO THE KING

THE UNBELIEVABLE MR. BROWNSTONE™ BOOK EIGHT

MICHAEL ANDERLE

HAIL TO THE KING TEAM


**Special Thanks**
to Mike Ross
for BBQ Consulting
Jessie Rae's BBQ - Las Vegas, NV

**Thanks to the JIT Readers**

Daniel Weigert
Peter Manis
John Ashmore
James Caplan
Kelly O'Donnell
Tim Bischoff
Larry Omans
Micky Cocker

*If I've missed anyone, please let me know!*

**Editor**
Lynne Stiegler

*To Family, Friends and*
*Those Who Love*
*to Read.*
*May We All Enjoy Grace*
*to Live the Life We Are*
*Called.*

No one liked a frowning cop, especially a criminal like Tyler. An angry cop from the LAPD Anti-Enhanced Threat Team was even worse. Without the AET the Black Sun's neutrality would vanish when the first violent asshole with an ego walked through the door, and given the place's clientele, that would take exactly two minutes.

Tyler sat across from the frowning Maria Hall at a table in the corner. The AET lieutenant sipped a beer, her frown sometimes turning into an outright scowl. She'd been quiet since strolling in, which was why he'd offered to chat with her at a table rather than the bar. He didn't need her exploding at someone until he knew the situation. One punch from a drunk thug and AET would swarm the Black Sun.

*Need to get this shit figured out before I end up with a nasty surprise.*

Tyler forced a smile onto his face. "Problem, Lieutenant?"

The cop took a long draw of her beer before answering. "It's annoying when you think you have shit figured out but then everything changes. Not just annoying, frustrating. I'm not a damned rookie. I shouldn't be making rookie mistakes."

Tyler shrugged. "Everyone's wrong now and again. Even me, on rare occasions."

"Sure, but they don't throw a lot of resources and time at their mistakes, and I have." Maria set her beer down. "Plus, once you make a mistake, it makes you think about other shit, and that messes with you. Maybe I'm pissed about all these new questions bothering me."

"What questions?"

The cop continued staring at her glass for a few seconds before replying, "About how I might be wrong about a bunch of things, and as a cop, that's not a feeling I like having."

Tyler chuckled. "Having some sort of crisis of conscience?"

Maria looked up. "I guess you could call it something like that." She looked at the bartender and shrugged.

"I figure if you're not dead, you can always fix it going forward. What were you wrong about?"

"Brownstone." The lieutenant locked eyes with Tyler.

*No, no, no. Say ain't it so, Lieutenant. Your hatred of Brownstone was the thing I liked about you the most.*

Tyler groaned and scrubbed his face with a hand. "No, you're right about him. He's still a power-hungry douchebag who doesn't give a shit about anyone but himself. Fuck Brownstone with a rusty two-by-four."

"How do you have a rusty piece of wood?" Maria laughed.

"You know what I mean."

Maria shrugged. "The point is it took me a while, but I get that he's just a guy trying to move things along the only way he knows how. I know you two don't see eye to eye, but think about it. If Brownstone really had it in for you this place would be a crater. Busting down your door was nothing, and he even paid for that."

*A crater? It might still be. Brownstone's gonna get me back for my little practical joke with his groupies. He might have gotten lucky with those freaks erasing the video, but he still blames me. I know he does.*

"Easy for you to say." Tyler pointed at her shield. "You're a cop. Brownstone doesn't fuck with cops."

"Yeah, you're right. He's gone out of his way to communicate with the cops when shit's going down." Maria glanced down at her uniform and then nodded before looking up. "And I've been a petty, jealous little bitch about the whole thing. Brownstone's saved a lot of lives by taking down high-level assholes, and I have to respect him for that."

"No, you don't. I'm still firmly in the 'Fuck Brownstone' club." Tyler shook his head. "This is one of those things where we're just going to have to agree to disagree, Lieutenant."

"Maria." She tapped her name tape on her uniform. "Think we're past the Lieutenant Hall stage of things."

"Huh?" Tyler blinked a few times, confused.

"I hang out here enough and I call you by your name, so why don't you call me by mine?" She shrugged. "You've done it a few times, but mostly you call me Lieutenant or Hall, so let's make this a little less formal even if I'm not a member of the 'Fuck Brownstone' club anymore. Friends can disagree about stuff."

Some subtle emotion flickered across her face, but Tyler couldn't place it. His stomach tightened.

*Shit. What's going on here? Does she have the hots for Brownstone? I could handle a lot of shit, but not that. Anything but that.*

The bartender returned her shrug. "Okay, Maria. Fine by me."

She reached into her pocket to pull out a business card and tossed it in front of him.

Tyler picked up the card. It was for the Seven Hills, a ritzy and exclusive Italian place that he'd heard of. He'd never been able to score a reservation there.

He eyed the card. "What's this about? AET going to raid the Seven Hills?"

Maria gestured toward the card. "It's got a date and time on the back. I'm inviting you to dinner. So unless you decide to do something highly illegal during our meal, there won't be any cop shit going down."

Tyler picked up the card and stared at it like it was some bizarre Oriceran scroll. "Dinner?"

The cop snorted. "Yeah, you know, the thing where two people eat at night? They often dress up. It might be nice to eat in a place with you that has something a little more substantial than pretzels."

"Oh. Sure, I guess. That sounds fine." Tyler glanced behind him at a pretzel bowl on the bar.

Maria stood. "Anyway, I've got to get going. See you around, Tyler."

"See you around, Maria." He gave her a polite nod, hoping she couldn't see how confused he was.

Tyler sat there and stared at the retreating woman as she made her way out of the Black Sun, still stunned and having trouble processing what had just happened. If he didn't know any better, he'd think the tough cop had just asked him, a criminal information broker, on a date at a fancy restaurant.

*Nah, this isn't a date. It's something else. Maybe she just wants to talk about Dannec or some shit.*

*But that doesn't make any sense. If she did, we could just talk in my office.*

Tyler groaned. It *was* a date.

*Shit. How does this work? Am I supposed to pay, or does she? She's the one who asked me out. Fuck, that place is expensive. Maybe we'll split the bill?*

Tyler shook his head. He was getting ahead of himself. He couldn't go on a date with her. It wasn't that Maria wasn't good enough. She had a good head on her shoulders and a hot athletic body even if he didn't get to see it on display under her uniform. Even if she'd fallen off the Brownstone hate train, she'd at least understood where Tyler was coming from before, which meant she understood him on some level.

*No, I can't do this. Date a cop? Even if she's playing fast and loose with Dannec, she's still a cop, and this shit will end badly. She'll start thinking I'm a piece of shit and stop enforcing the neutrality at the Black Sun. Then I'm fucked.*

He groaned and ran his hands through his hair. Several

nearby patrons glanced at him with confused looks on their faces.

"What the fuck is wrong?" he shouted. "Never seen an annoyed man before? Drink your fucking booze and look somewhere else."

They returned their attention to their drinks, several cursing under their breath.

*It's just a date. It's not like she said she wants to marry my ass or fuck me. I can do this. I should do this.*

Tyler forced himself to his feet. "How can I be an info broker if I don't know the info and have the contacts?" he muttered to himself. "If I turn her down, she's going to be pissed with me."

The words came out of his mouth and he believed them, but the dread pricking his stomach and heart wouldn't leave.

Sergeant Weber was finishing up a report when Matthews strolled up to his desk. The AET officer looked around before leaning toward Weber.

"What the fuck is up with Hall?" Matthews whispered, resting his arm, palm-down, on Weber's desk. "You're practically her secretary, so you should know."

The sergeant looked up from his computer. "Huh? What do you mean? She seems fine to me, and I've been getting her coffee all day."

"She's also been smirking all day like she knows some shit we don't know. Something obviously happened last night." Matthews winked. "Come on, we both know the only time she's that happy is when she's ready to drop the boom on someone. I'm not sure who's in the shitter, but it's got to be someone, and I'm just hoping it's no one on the team." A chuckle and a huge grin followed.

Weber shook his head. "She's happy with how everything went down with those Drow. Hell, she's even happy with Brownstone, and he's been the target of her hate for a while now." He swiveled his chair to face the other man. "Look, she thought the captain and the mayor were going to ride her ass about getting the National Guard involved, but they both went off about how she showed great initiative, and as far as I know, the consulate had been helping her track the guys. All the brass are happy, so why wouldn't she be?" He shrugged.

Matthews frowned. "Then what is it?" He stood up straight and crossed his arms.

The sergeant shrugged. "Who knows? Maybe she has a date."

They stared at each other for a few seconds before bursting into loud laughter.

Matthews slapped his knee. "Yeah, whatever. The only thing the Lieutenant would ever date is a railgun."

* * *

Charlyce whistled to herself as she folded clothes on the couch. There was nothing like fresh-from-the-dryer clothes: nice warmth and good smell. She wished she could do more for the orphans that day than help with their laundry, but Father McCartney had stressed to her that *everything* she was doing was helpful.

*I'm useful. I was useful to no one for so many years, and now Trey needs me. The kids need me.*

Father McCartney strolled into the room with a broad smile on his face and his phone in his hand.

Charlyce finished folding a small green shirt and placed it on a pile before looking at the priest. "You look happy, Father."

The priest shrugged. "It's always helpful to be reminded of the goodness of people. Your weekly assistance is a continuing example of that, as are donations. Our anonymous donor has struck again with a particularly large donation." He held up the phone for a few seconds before pocketing it. "He just let me know. Or maybe she. I don't know their true identity."

"That's wonderful to hear." Charlyce let out a contented sigh and shook her head. "I wonder if it's an orphan who has fond memories of this place."

"Perhaps." Father McCartney furrowed his brow, then shrugged. "I thought it might be James, and he *has* donated a lot of money to this place, but when I asked him about it he pointed out that he has no reason to hide donations."

Charlyce nodded. "I don't see why Mr. Brownstone would hide like that." She grabbed her purse from the small table in front of her and fished out five twenties.

She stood and offered the money, but looked down at the ground. "I know that it's not as much as Mr. Brownstones gives or the other donor, but I want to do my part. Not just by being here, but helping you, just like you're helping all the kids here."

Father McCartney accepted the money with a warm

smile and took a few steps back. "You misunderstand the value of donations, Charlyce."

She sighed and sat back down. "I know. This money ain't worth much. It's an insult to what you're doing."

"No, no, no. Not at all." The priest waved a hand. "A wealthy man who gives soup to another sacrifices little, unlike a man who is half-starving. It isn't the size of a gift that's important, but the heart of the person who gives it." He pointed to his heart. "The heart of the man who gives a large check is no better and no worse than yours. You're both giving us what you can afford, and I appreciate the electricity, water, or food your donation will provide us."

Charlyce lifted her head, her smile returning. "Thank you for your kind words, Father, but I still don't know. I've been taking a Currus here. I could be spending that money on the kids."

"You have to get here somehow, and a minor luxury for a woman spending most of her free time volunteering isn't outrageous, even by the standards of a priest. You're not a nun, Charlyce."

"I ain't even Catholic." She laughed.

Father McCartney chuckled. "No one's perfect except our Lord. Just know that *all* your contributions here are valued." He glanced at the clock, and his smile faded. "I have to go give someone a call, so I'll talk to you later."

"See you around, Father." Charlyce waved.

The priest offered her a final nod before continuing out of the room.

Charlyce returned to the couch.

Meaning. That was what her life had lacked before, and now she had more family, friends, and people to protect.

*Thank you, Lord, for giving me this second chance.*

---

The consul sighed and rubbed the bridge of his nose. The king wanted an answer, and diplomatic dissembling wouldn't work.

*Damned Drow. Why couldn't you have just listened? Your arrogance will lead to suffering for all of us, you fools.*

The Light Elf cleared his throat and looked at the image of his King sitting at an ornate desk on Oriceran hanging in the air. "Your Highness, this latest incident concerns me. I was able to cover up the Drow's previous rabblerousing, but there was no way I was going to be able to do it this time."

"Which was why you provided information to the human authorities?" The king's face remained impassive, but his crossed arms and rigid posture said enough.

The consul took a deep breath and slowly let it out. "I don't regret any of that, and the Drow's subsequent actions only proved how dangerous they were. Going after this Brownstone was one thing, but opening far-dimensional portals?" He shook his head. "I suspect every magical being in this region felt what they did."

"Laena has gone too far," the king replied, his face tight. He uncrossed his arms. "She's pushed well past any acceptable lines with her efforts."

The consul nodded. "So how are we to react to these provocations?" He relaxed his fists, having not even realized he'd clenched them.

"Remember, we shouldn't be like the Drow, hasty and foolish." The king looked to the side and sighed.

"What do you mean? This deserves an answer." He gestured around him. "If we do nothing they will think they can get away with anything, and more incidents will follow, Your Highness. More people will die, and the human authorities will begin to blame others, maybe even us. The situation is tenuous enough as it is." His fingers threatened to curl into fists again, but he resisted.

The king shook his head. "We must think long-term, not short-term. Yes, you're right. The situation between Earth and Oriceran is precarious enough as it is, and that's before any of the more disturbing aspects of what the Seer's Quatrains imply about our world are considered. Still, we can't risk starting a war with the Drow."

The consul let out another weary sigh. "I'd say *they* are the ones starting a war."

The king shook his head. "No, they are launching foolish attacks, and these foolish attacks have cost them their lives, for the most part. I'm content to give Laena a small amount of time to consider the implications of her failures. She might be ruthless and arrogant, but she's far from foolish." He stood.

"Are you sure, Your Highness?" The consul placed his arms behind his back, to give them something to do that wouldn't betray his nervousness to the king.

The king nodded gravely. "If we war against the Drow it'll come to Earth, and if the war lands on Earth, we might as well blow up our planet ourselves."

"I can see your wisdom in this, but I still feel we should do something."

"And what would you suggest?" The king arched a brow.

The consul dipped his head for a moment in thought. "At the minimum, Laena should be made aware that we're watching her. That might constrain the Drow's future actions." He looked back up. "Since she's no longer here, perhaps someone on the Oriceran side could leave an official strongly-worded message kindly suggesting that it'd be best if the queen does not show up on Earth again anytime soon."

The king nodded. "I'll see that it's taken care of. If the Drow return to Earth, inform me immediately."

The consul bowed his head. "As you wish, Your Highness."

2

---

Shay leaned forward on the couch and eyed James' chest as he sat in a chair across from her. "You should have brought the Whispering Amulet of Doom."

*I've got too many doom artifacts in my life lately.*

James grunted. "You've already seen it. Not like we need it here to talk about it." He looked away, discomfort etched on his face. He was starting to regret having told Shay about the recent change.

"But you just told me you can talk to it now." Shay rolled her eyes. "You can't drop something like that on me and then try to act like it's no big deal."

James shook his head. "I didn't say I could talk to it, just that I'm starting to understand it some. Most of that was more about knowing what it was feeling than what it was saying."

Shay laughed. "So you're saying you do a better job of understanding your amulet than me?"

"Something like that, yeah." James shrugged.

Shay leaned back and looked James up and down. "The

more you can communicate with it, the greater the potential to unlock more of its power."

"That's if it has more."

"Oh, I bet it does, but the armor is nice enough."

"Yeah." James nodded. "Be dead ten times over without it."

"You said you figured out how it worked?" Shay tilted her head slightly, a pained expression on her face. "Or did the amulet tell you?"

James shook his head. "No, I figured it out. It's obvious now that the thing adapts after attacks." He gestured toward his chest. "It's not perfect, but after the first hit, it'll make me more resistant to that type of attack. It's like it knows what to watch for."

It was good to have some small advance in understanding. He'd gone so many years having no clue what the amulet represented, and even worried that it was infernal. Now he not only knew it was alien in origin but was closer to understanding its true nature.

Shay tapped her bottom lip. "Kind of like a vaccine, then?"

"Yeah."

Shay blew out a breath and stood. "But it's really specific in some ways. You've been hit with magic before, and it didn't protect you at first against the Drow." She started pacing.

"I don't think it's as general as magic or non-magic." James shrugged. "I've been stabbed with swords before, and it didn't help me when that Harriken fuck used the Masamune on me." He ran his hand over his chest and down his stomach, remembering the pain of the wound. "I don't know if it's the material or the spell, but I'm guessing it's like the specific type of energy, magical or not. Maybe I'm resistant to shadow magic now. Don't know."

"That would make sense." Shay stopped pacing and closed on James, her eyes narrowed.

He looked up at her uncertainly.

*Shit. What's going on in her head? Whatever the next sentence is, I'm guessing it won't be good.*

She tapped his chest. "I'm going to need to shoot you."

*Yeah, not good.*

"Huh?" James rose slowly, his hands in front of his chest. He didn't understand women all that well, and the relationship podcast hadn't covered what to say if your girlfriend said she wanted to shoot you.

"So it can learn." Shay shrugged. "The Whispering Amulet of Doom."

"Oh. Yeah, that makes sense." James dropped his hands and shook his head. "Bullets are fine. I've been using it so long that it's already adapted to a lot of things."

Shay nodded. "I guess that's true. I've seen you take tons of bullets, knives, and shotgun pellets. You've been burned by fire that would have sent other people to the hospital." She winced.

"Yeah, I figure bullets and pellets are kind of the same thing." He settled back into his chair. "Bullets, in the end, are just about applying kinetic energy."

Shay shook her head. "We still don't know if it's that general."

James frowned. "What do you mean?"

"It's alien shit that may or may not be magical." Shay pulled open her jacket to reveal a sheath for one of the magical gnomish knives. "And being magical can make a big difference, even if it's functionally the same on the surface. For all we know, it could be as specific as 'protect James from metal bullets made from lead.' Someone might roll up and shoot you with a silver bullet or something, and you go down."

The bounty hunter shrugged. "Yeah. Maybe. I'm not gonna say I never get surprised like with the Harriken sword."

She snapped her fingers. "I just thought of something. I'm so fucking brilliant."

"What?"

"You should ask it." Shay pointed to his chest.

"The amulet?"

She nodded. "Yeah. If you understand more of it now, maybe it'll answer."

"I don't know." James frowned and looked down. "It wasn't responding to my thoughts from what I could tell, but to the situation, and I'm still not sure if me understanding more of what it's saying is good or bad." He looked back up. "This thing fuses with my body. For all I know, it might be able to take control of me."

A strange look passed over Shay's face for a moment.

James frowned. "What?"

Shay waved a hand. "Nothing, just…thinking, was all. It'd be helpful if we knew more about where you came from, but I can look into that."

"Yeah." James grunted. "I'm not good at the research shit."

Shay smiled, though it seemed forced.

*She's probably freaked out by having all this alien shit up in her face. Can't blame her.*

"What do we do in the meantime?" James asked.

Shay shrugged. "We train it."

"Train it?"

"Yeah. If we don't know how far it goes with bullets, we shoot you with different guns."

James grunted. "And we're back to shooting me."

Shay laughed. "Yeah, just go to that witch of yours and stock up on healing potions if you're worried."

"Those things aren't cheap."

"The more you're immune to, the less you'll have to use them in the future." Shay settled back on the couch and crossed her legs. "Think of it as an investment."

James nodded. "Okay, fine." He sighed. "Part one of the plan is shooting me a lot."

"Yeah." Shay grinned. "I'm only suggesting this for your own good."

The bounty hunter grunted. "Yeah, yeah. And what else?"

"Beat you with different weapons. Stab you." Shay whipped out her knife and sliced the air a few times. "Try and fry you different ways. Sonic attacks. There's a lot of shit we could do." She grinned.

James eyed her for a few seconds before speaking. "You look like you're enjoying the idea of trying to hurt me way too much."

Shay winked. "Oh, no. It's all for your own good, James." Her eyes widened, and her mouth formed an O. "Maybe a harpoon?"

"A harpoon?"

"Yeah, you ever been harpooned?" She mimicked throwing a harpoon. "I've used one a few times."

"No. I'm not a fucking shark or a whale." James snorted.

Shay laughed. "Just saying, you never know what you'll need to deal with bounty-wise. We need to be systematic about this, including testing shit we think you might already be immune to, like most rifles, pistols, and shotguns." Her smile widened. "Might want to work on small-dose toxins and shit, too." She rubbed her hands together.

James shook his head. "I'm not letting you fucking poison me."

Shay put her thumb and forefinger together. "Just a little. How will we know if it works otherwise?"

"I'll live with the mystery."

Shay rolled her eyes. "Until some poison mage kills you."

James gave her a broad grin and shook his head. "I'd just kill him before he could do that."

---

Laena frowned down at the kneeling Drow from her throne. "Rise and report."

"Yes, My Queen." The Drow stood. "We've verified what happened to the three you sent to Earth. They're dead."

She snorted. "I know that already. What I need to know are the circumstances of their demise. That will influence everything going forward."

"The same humans who slew Widowmaker aided Brownstone against the three." His hands hung loosely at this side, trembling slightly.

"I see," she hissed. "They are proving more resourceful than I imagined." She rubbed her chin. "A failure of imagination perhaps."

"We've been able to verify that Brownstone himself is quite powerful." The Drow messenger swallowed. "Although we don't know the source of his power. Some of the magical signatures in the area are strange. They are like nothing we've ever encountered." His face tensed as if he expected the queen to strike him down.

Laena did no such thing. Instead, she merely nodded and leaned against the back of her throne. "The human found himself a special trinket, I suspect. We've underestimated him, to our loss."

"My Queen?" The Drow glanced behind him as if he expected someone else to be there.

The queen didn't care if he understood. She would *make* him understand, and even if he didn't, he only needed to deliver her words to others.

"Widowmaker was arrogant and depraved." Laena flicked her wrist. "It didn't surprise me that she was defeated, but Zavan and his subordinates lacked her flaws. For them to be defeated proves that Brownstone and his allies are worthy of respect. Continuing to throw more Drow at him on Earth will result in unnecessary sacrifices." She threw out her arm in a grand gesture.

The man blinked a few times, confusion written all over his face. "What are we to do, then?"

Laena shrugged a single shoulder. "Nothing." She settled back onto her throne.

"Nothing?"

"We shall pause." The queen gave a pained sigh. "This

will also resolve our problems with the Light Elves. They keep whining about our efforts on Earth. They are too cowardly to do anything about it at the moment, but if we push them, they may rediscover they have a backbone." She frowned and shook her head. "We've been fortunate that the Fixer hasn't involved himself in our efforts yet. The more we push, the greater the chance we play to their advantages on Earth."

"So we give up?" Something like a defiant frown appeared on the Drow's face, but he withered under the queen's glare, and his trembling became more pronounced

"No," she barked, her hand still raised and thoughts of magical punishment lingering. "As I said, we pause. This Brownstone might have a powerful trinket and friends, but he's still human. We've let rumors and prophecies push us into hasty action." She lowered her hand and rested it on her lap. "We're panicking like short-lived humans when we should be conducting ourselves as proud Drow. We live longer, so we should think long-term."

The man swallowed before speaking. "Are you sure this is…a wise course of action? What about the wish?"

"I doubt they even know about the wish." Laena nodded. "The more I think about this, the more convinced I become of that. There is no way a human could resist using the wish if they knew about it. Our legacy and future are secure. No matter what strange mutterings have left the mouths of the Seers Oriceran might never suffer a dismal fate, and even if it does, it won't happen in mere weeks or months."

"And what of the Princess?"

Laena glanced toward several dark-shadow scrying orbs floating in the corner of the room. "James Brownstone has her hidden somewhere that we can't easily track, which means she's safe from others who might track her. It's not like it matters if we wait a few months or a few years. We shall allow the others to go back to their petty day-to-day lives and forget that we even had an interest in them." She squeezed her hand into a fist. "And then, when they've let their guard down, we can track and find the princess. She will leave the protection of Brownstone's allies, and we shall seize what is ours."

James grunted and rose from his chair. "I'm not gonna try and get struck by lightning on purpose."

"Are you running away?" Shay snorted.

"No, I just wanted a sandwich. But that doesn't change what I just said."

Shay rolled her eyes. "I was saying you should build up to that with lower amounts of electricity, not start out with the lightning, you big baby. You're acting like you don't even have a Whispering Amulet of Doom."

Someone knocked on the door and she tensed, her hand reaching for the gun she didn't have on her. It was hanging in the holster in the bedroom. Her fingers drifted to her knife's hilt.

James stepped over to the couch to pat her on the shoulder. "My house is safe."

"Really?" Shay scoffed, shrugged off his hand and stood, her hand still inside her jacket. "Your last house got blown up by a rocket launcher. Kind of hard to forget, even if you don't have a photographic memory."

"Yeah, but they didn't knock first." James shrugged, grinning, and went to the door.

No gangsters or terrorists stood on James' porch. It was Sergeant Mack. Shay dropped her hand.

The men shook hands before the cop spoke. "Sorry to bother you." He glanced at Shay. "Had some stuff I wanted to talk to you about, but I didn't realize you had company."

Shay walked over and kissed James on the cheek. "I need to get going anyway. I still have to do my daily workout."

Sergeant Mack frowned. "Don't leave on my account."

"Nah, you're just a convenient excuse." She winked and turned to James. "Keep what we were talking about in mind."

James grunted and shook his head. "No means no."

Shay smirked as she headed into the bedroom to grab her coat and holster and left. Mack remained quiet until the woman had gone out the front and closed the door behind her.

Mack clucked his tongue. "Don't let her boss you around, Brownstone. My woman's always trying to force me into boring-ass things that she likes, and I don't. A good relationship's about knowing when to just let the other person be and when you have to push back." He mimed a pushing motion to emphasize his statement.

"You don't know Shay." James stared at the door, half-convinced she'd kick it down and suggest some new extreme amulet test.

Mack laughed. "Maybe not, but I know strong-willed

women. Men like us need strong women. Normal women can't keep up with us."

James stepped toward the kitchen. "I was about to make a sandwich. Want one?"

Mack frowned. "Nah. I'm fine."

"You don't like sandwiches?" James stopped.

The cop shook his head. "Not hungry. It's got nothing to do with that."

"What's wrong?"

"Just one of those weird coincidences." The cop shrugged.

"Weird coincidences?" James turned around to face Mack.

"Yeah." The sergeant glanced toward the closed front door. "There's a woman who kind of looks like Shay, or maybe younger. She's been running around doing parkour in the evenings."

James nodded slowly. "Nothing wrong with parkour though, right?"

"Well, not in and of itself, no. But this woman's been bouncing through a lot of private property and restricted areas. It's the trespassing, not the parkour, that's gonna get her in trouble." He shrugged. "Of course someone has to catch her first, and the way she's moving, it's not like any of us cops are going to pull it off. Even AET can't move like that."

*Shit. Shay needs to be more careful, especially since she just got Hall off her back. Wonder if I need to do something about this?*

James grunted, consumed by worry, his appetite gone. "That's LA for you. All sorts of freaks."

"Yeah, the weird thing is, although we've got some video from security cameras and that sort of thing, there's a lot of other videos that have been sent to the station that don't seem to be from security cameras." Mack looked to the side for a moment as if he were trying to picture the videos in his mind. "Some from rooftops, so not just random people seeing something weird."

"'If you see something, say something' and all that."

"Yeah, probably." Mack waved a hand and nodded toward the couch. "May I sit? I didn't come to talk about parkour women. I came to talk about something much more important."

"What's that?" James nodded toward the couch.

The sergeant sat down. "Barbeque and our team. We need to start talking about equipment, specifically our main pit."

James decided to return to his lounge chair now that he'd abandoned the sandwich plan. The chair didn't fit him like his old favorite did, but there wasn't a lot he could do about that.

*Thanks, rocket-launcher asshole.*

"What did you have in mind, Mack?" The bounty hunter shifted his body for a few seconds to get comfortable.

"Something huge." Mack pointed to the ceiling for a second before dropping his hand. "We need to show these fools that PFW is here to represent barbeque."

James nodded. "Yeah, and how do we do this?"

"Like I said, something huge. Something that shows we aren't afraid of anything." He pointed to himself and then James.

The bounty hunter gave him a quick nod. "I can get behind huge barbeque."

Mack grinned. "You know what? We should do a big-rig-sized pit."

"A big-rig-sized pit?"

The cop spread his hands in front of him. "Imagine this, Brownstone. Imagine if we built something so large we would have to use a Kenworth to pull it."

"Yeah," James rumbled, his eyes lighting up at the idea. "That would be fucking badass. We could make the entire county smell our barbeque."

James and Mack both laughed.

The bounty hunter sighed and shook his head. While the rest of his life might have ripped past any possibility of being constrained by his old KISS philosophy, there was no reason barbeque couldn't.

"But we need to be practical." James grunted and shrugged. "We need something my truck can handle. Not like we can always have a big rig around for competitions."

Mack sighed and nodded. "Guess you're right." He let his head drop against the back of the couch.

"I'll figure something out, but I need you to work on finding a good place to store our wood." James' gaze flicked toward his secured basement door. Good place for death-dealing tools, not so much for barbeque wood. "A place where we can keep it seasoned right and maintain good humidity. Not like we can make up for that shit once we've started cooking."

Mack waved a hand. "Don't worry. I think I already know a place." He grinned. "Hell, I can toss out my mother-in-law and use the room she's living in. I won't miss her."

The men shared another laugh.

"What would your wife say if she heard that?" James wondered.

"Something pretty loud and foul." Mack leaned forward to whisper, "Guess it's a good thing she's not here. Like I said before, men like us need strong women."

"Don't I know it! Hey, I got a question. You understand women? You understand your wife?"

Mack sat back up and shook his head. "I've been married a hell of a long time, and I don't think I'll ever understand any woman, let alone *my* woman. Not totally." He reached into his pocket to pull out a piece of paper. "But I do understand barbeque, and I wanted to talk about which boys we might want doing what."

James glanced out at the front, thinking about Shay.

*I've been trying so hard to understand her, but maybe I never will. Guess I'll just have to ride this shit out and see what happens. It feels good in the meantime.*

"Let's do it."

3

James allowed himself to smile as he appreciated the sheen of his polished kitchen counter. Shay might call it OCD, but he insisted it was nothing more than keeping his life simple. Food poisoning didn't make for a simple day.

He frowned, thinking over that explanation. He hadn't had food poisoning that he could remember, which meant every day after his earliest childhood years. Maybe the amulet, even when off, or his alien physiology somehow protected him.

His phone rang, and he pulled it out of his pocket.

"Hey, Shay," James answered.

"So I'm going to be heading off on a job for the Professor soon, but I wanted you to come over to Warehouse Three for a few tests before that."

"Tests?" James grimaced. He thought he knew what she was talking about, but maybe he was wrong.

Shay laughed. "Yeah, concerning your little whispering pal."

James grunted. "I don't think that'll be very helpful." He set the phone down and put it on speaker mode. Might as well get in some more polishing while they were chatting.

"Bullshit, it won't. Knowing the exact limits of your defenses means you can kick ass in a more tactically-sound way."

"I don't put that much thought into it." He grabbed his rag and spray bottle to head to the other end of the counter. "I kick ass and ask questions later."

James could almost hear the eye roll over the phone. "Sure, James. Sure. Just get your ass over here. Let me put it another way. I don't want to have to worry about your ass when I'm out on a job. I don't know if I can pull off getting my ass teleported back from overseas next time you're in trouble."

"Okay, okay. I'll come over soon. I've just got some shit to take care of." He squirted the bottle a few times and set it to the side.

Shay snickered. "Let me guess, you're polishing your already-ridiculously-clean counter, and you're going to dust a bunch of shit like a sixty-year-old Victorian maid."

"I've got some cleaning to do, yeah." James grunted and rubbed the rag on the counter.

"Just hurry it along there, Mr. Maid. See you soon." Shay hung up.

James frowned at the phone, then put his rag down, retrieved a pair of earbuds, placed them in, and started up a new podcast. It was *Grilling Satori*, which was focused on *yakiniku*. His first love would always be American barbeque, but his jaunt to Japan had opened his eyes to other grilled meat possibilities.

James reached for his rag as his phone rang again.

"Hold your damned horses, Shay."

When he pulled the phone out of his pocket, he chuckled. It was Alison, the other bossy woman in his life.

"Hey, kid, what's up?" James adjusted the phone so he could hear better.

"Hey, Dad. Just excited to be coming home soon."

James eyed the rag and decided to devote his full attention to talking to his daughter. "Regret taking on the special project?"

"No, no. Just it's been too long." Alison let out a wistful sigh. "Two weeks, and then we can spend most of the summer together."

James smiled. "Yeah, sounds good. I've been looking into concerts and sh…stuff we can go to together."

Alison let out a contented sigh. "Plus, if I'm there maybe I can keep you out of trouble."

"Out of trouble?" James stepped out of the kitchen so the rag wouldn't tempt him.

"I'm still upset about what happened with those Drow."

"It's fine, Alison. They're dead now, and with the AET and the consulate looking into things I doubt the Drow will try anything anytime soon."

James grunted and glanced at his door. Never knew when some magical asshole might kick it open.

"It's not just the Drow, though." She muttered something under her breath about kicking dark elf butt.

"What?" James dropped back into his lounge chair. "The Drow were the big deal."

"That stuff in Las Vegas, too. That was important."

"What about it? That wasn't anything special, just a

level four." His hands itched to do something. He hadn't realized he was so obsessed with multi-tasking.

"But I also know you didn't have your amulet."

James grunted. Shay must have passed that little piece of information about his confrontation with the Red-Eyes Killer along. Even though he'd brought up the existence of the amulet with the girl previously, he still wasn't sure if he felt comfortable with her knowing about it. It was just more crap the poor teenager had to worry about.

Still, it wasn't like he'd be able to keep many secrets from her. If she started asking too many questions when they were in the same room together during the summer, it'd only be a matter of time before she pushed and found out about his alien origin.

*What the fuck am I so afraid of? Alison's half-Drow. It's not like she's gonna be that freaked that her new dad isn't human.*

"I didn't need my amulet for a level four, and I had a healing potion with me," James rumbled.

"A healing potion isn't going to do anything if you're dead," Alison snapped. "I read about that Red-Eyes Killer online. He was cutting people's heads off."

*Yeah, and then I cut his head off.*

James smirked and extended his footrest. Might as well get comfortable. "I took him out okay."

"And you got lucky with the Drow because you knew they were coming. If they had ambushed you at home or something without your amulet you'd be dead."

James grunted. "Like I said, they weren't a problem."

"I want you to make me a promise, Dad. A promise that will make me feel a lot better about all this."

"Sure, kid, anything."

"Wear the amulet all the time from now on."

James' heart rate kicked up. He'd been expecting her to ask him to be more careful.

"What the… Alison, I don't think that's a good idea. That thing has weird side-effects."

"Big deal," Alison shot back, heaving another long sigh. "All magic does. So, what, you want me to wear the Aegis Pendant all the time to protect myself, but you're not going to wear the amulet?"

Stubborn Drow teenagers were worse than Drow assassins.

"It's not the same thing." James groaned and rubbed his temple with his free hand.

Alison sniffled. "You don't get it, do you?"

*Oh, shit. Is she crying? Fuck.* Damn it.

"I… Alison, I'm careful."

"I bet my mom was careful, too, and she still ended up dead."

James sighed and let his head fall back against the chair. Alison had suffered so much, and shouldn't have to spend her time stressing over him.

*I'm a shitty dad.*

It didn't help that Alison was right. She was in the middle of a government-sponsored magic school, surrounded by powerful creatures, witches, and wizards who could protect her. The fact that the Drow had targeted him instead of her proved that the School of Necessary Magic was a safe place, but he still felt better about her wandering around if she wore her Aegis Pendant.

Unlike Alison, James also made a point of going after dangerous people, and Vegas had proved that he wasn't always ready for trouble. If the Red-Eyes Killer had been tougher he would have had to drive all the way back to Los Angeles to get his stuff, and more people might have died.

Alison's sniffles broke into full sobs on the other end. James' stomach tightened, and his free hand went to his forehead.

"Okay," he muttered into the phone.

"Okay?" Alison echoed after another sob.

James lowered the phone and stared at it for a few seconds before lifting back to his ear. "I'll do it. I'll start wearing the amulet all the time. Maybe not to bed, but I'll have it always near me at least."

The teen regained control after a few more sniffles. "Thanks, Dad. That's all I ask."

*Guess I'm gonna get used to hearing weird-ass alien whispers. Hope the amulet likes barbeque.*

"I forgot to tell you, the adoption will be finalized in July." He managed a smile despite the discomfort just moments earlier.

"Then I'll officially be Alison Brownstone." Happiness infected her voice.

"Yeah, sucks to be you."

Alison let out a little laugh, which relieved James.

"Everything's only been getting better," the girl responded. "And I'm sure it's only going to get even better from here on."

"I'm sure it will, Alison. I'm sure it will. Hey, why don't you tell me the cool stuff that's been going on at your school?"

Alison sucked in a deep breath as if she were about to

unleash paragraphs in seconds. "Well, first of all, Izzie did the funniest thing the other day…"

———

An hour later, James' F-350 roared down the highway toward Warehouse Three. He'd stopped by his own more modest "warehouse" to pick up the amulet.

*A storage unit's been good enough for years. It's not like I should change just because Shay has a bunch of actual warehouses.*

*I also can't believe I'm gonna go to Shay's place and let her shoot me.*

The amulet whispered in his mind, amused by the idea.

*Glad one of us is gonna enjoy it. Is this your idea of entertainment?*

It didn't respond. James still wasn't sure if the communication was one-way, but because of Alison's new requirement, he'd find out soon enough. He wasn't sure if he'd wear it constantly or just have it with him, but it was at least a good experiment to try.

Finding out that the amulet was of alien origin rather than magical had done a lot to soothe his concerns. He figured the devil would rely on something a little less elaborate if he were trying to take James' soul. At least he hoped so.

*Maybe if I wear this shit all the time, it'll eventually get tired of talking. For now, I'll do what I need to, because if I get killed, Alison might not be safe even at the school. I have to remember that I'm not just living for myself anymore. I'm living for two wonderful women.*

James frowned. He needed to protect his women any way he could.

"Fuck. That parkour shit has to be Shay, and if I tell her to knock it off, she'll just call me a name and do it twice as often to make a point. Maybe I can handle it in a different way."

He waited until he was sure no one would pass him soon to hit "Heather" in his contacts list and turned on the speakerphone.

The phone rang once. "Verify identity," a distorted voice demanded.

"James Brownstone." He checked his mirrors to make sure there were no suspicious vehicles.

"Confirm the first job."

James returned his attention to the front. "You know the fucking first job."

"Confirm the first job," the voice repeated.

"I needed you to take care of some video of some women hanging on me in a bar."

The distorted voice laughed. "Give me a real challenge this time, Mr. Brownstone," Heather continued, her voice undistorted this time.

The bounty hunter grunted. "I don't know if it's a real challenge, but it's important to me."

"What's up, Mr. Brownstone?"

"A woman is parkouring around Los Angeles at night. She sometimes goes places she shouldn't."

"Oh, she'll be easy to track."

"I don't want her tracked." James paused for a moment as he changed lanes. "I'm more concerned about video of her. Most of it is security-cam shit, but there's some other video that seems a little more directed. I want you to find out who is filming it, and then we can talk about if I need it taken down."

Heather chuckled. "Sure thing. This will be even easier than what you had me do before."

"Fine by me. Wait, don't you need the description of the woman?" James glanced around the cab, wondering if the hacker could somehow see him.

"Nope. What you've told me should be enough. By the way, I'm now burning this number."

"Huh? What the fuck are you talking about?" James slowed to let someone from the onramp in.

"You won't be able to get hold of me using this number."

"Then how the fuck am I supposed to talk to you about the job?" James shook his head.

"Don't worry, I'll call you." Heather hung up.

"Fucking hackers."

---

Guns arranged roughly by caliber and type lined several tables stretching across the interior of the main room of Warehouse Three. Shay stood behind the first table with a satisfied look on her face. The amulet continued its happy murmuring.

Shay eyed James. "Please tell me you've got it on. It'd be pretty damned embarrassing if I ended up killing you."

"Embarrassing? Yeah, I guess that's one way to put it." James patted his chest. "It's under here, and it's ready to go."

"Good. The more we know, the longer you live." The

tomb raider picked up a small .22 pistol from the first table. "Look, I figure we escalate this shit slowly and systematically. We know you can handle a lot of weapons, so as long as we up the power slowly we won't seriously injure you."

James snorted. "You *think* you won't."

Shay winked. "I don't think, I know. Don't be a pussy."

"You're not the one getting shot."

She narrowed her eyes and aimed the gun at his leg. "I'll keep it away from anything important, or anything I need to use later tonight."

The amulet whispered, eagerness in its mental voice.

James shrugged. "Whatever. Guess I should have worn shorts. Don't care that much about these pants, at least."

Shay pulled the trigger. The bullet bounced off with a faint sting and dropped to the ground.

"That all you got?" James rumbled, and squared his shoulders.

The tomb raider laughed. "Oh, so we go from all your complaints to you talking shit?" She set the .22 down and picked up a .357. "I guess I better up my game, Mr. Brownstone."

James moved his head back and forth and cracked his knuckles. The amulet's eagerness might have been infectious, or maybe he liked the idea of impressing his woman.

He nodded. "Do it."

The handgun spat out a bullet. It stung more than last time but didn't pierce the skin. Shay set the gun down, walked over to the bullets, and knelt.

"Huh," she murmured.

James glanced down at the two new holes in his pants, then at Shay. "What?"

She held up one of the bullets. "It's crushed like it hit a wall."

"Yeah, so?"

"Look, we don't know the exact mechanics of how all this shit works." Shay shook her head. "Alien or magical stuff might work in ways we can't even begin to understand, but this shows that the actual force of the bullet isn't shunted off to some weird other place. Otherwise, this wouldn't be messed up."

James shrugged. "Good to know, I guess."

Shay rolled her eyes. "A little curiosity never killed anyone."

"What about the cat?"

"The cat should have had better skills." Shay gestured toward the pistol table. "Maybe if it did, it wouldn't have ended up dead." She moved to the next table and picked up a 9mm submachine gun. She flipped the safety off and aimed at the same leg. "Has it even hurt you?"

"Stings a little, but nothing bad." James patted his leg where the bullets had struck. "Doesn't even hurt now."

Shay nodded. "Gonna use a burst."

"Fine by me."

The gunfire echoed in the cavernous warehouse. The bounty hunter grunted from the three quick spikes of pain. The bullets had managed a slight scrape, but no blood.

She set down the submachine gun. "I wonder what would happen with good stuff."

"Good stuff?" James furrowed his brow.

Shay nodded. "Yeah, like a healing potion."

"Don't have one on me, but I've used healing potions with the amulet on before. It didn't block the effects." James shrugged. "Also didn't seem like the healing was faster, but it wasn't like I was timing it or anything. Maybe the potions worked better than they would have otherwise."

The amulet whispered something. It sounded irritated.

*What? Don't like it when I use magic? Hurt your little alien ego? Fuck you. If you're so good, you should be healing me, asshole.*

The amulet grew silent. James wasn't sure if it was chance or reaction.

Shay set down the gun and moved to a table far down the line. She picked up a familiar sword, the Masamune *tachi.*

The amulet shouted in James' mind, eager and annoyed.

James grunted. "Yeah, this ought to be fun."

Shay gripped the hilt of the sword tightly. "You've already been hit so your amulet should have already adapted, right?"

The bounty hunter shrugged and lifted an arm to the side. "I'd rather lose an arm than a leg if we're wrong."

His sword-wielding girlfriend advanced with too broad a smile on her face, raising the sword. "Ready?"

James nodded. "Do it. Make it quick. No one likes a lazy hack job."

Shay brought the sword down, but it bounced off. It left a slight scratch with a thin trail of blood, and the amulet did its best mental imitation of something James thought was supposed to be laughter.

*Oh, you think you're big shit now? It would have helped when the fucker stabbed me the first time.*

Shay returned the sword to the table and picked up a stun gun. "Ever been hit with a stun gun or a Taser?"

"Yeah, tons of times. Low-level bounties use them all the time." He shrugged. "The first guy who tried got away. After that, it's been fun to see the looks on their faces."

"I'd use a Taser, but I don't think the probes will even work." Shay advanced on James, the stun gun crackling. "This will let us test electricity. Until we work up to lightning, at least."

"Yeah, whatever." James grunted. "Go ahead."

Shay jammed the stun gun into his side. A slight tingle traveled through James, but his muscles didn't contract and no pain shot through him.

"Tickles." James smirked.

Shay rolled her eyes. "Very funny." She moved back to the table. She set the stun gun down before picking up a small silver egg with a button on the side.

James eyed the egg. "Sonic grenade?"

"Yep. Been hit with one of these before?"

"Once, a few years back." He let out a low growl. "Fucker got away."

The amulet muttered something. Sympathy, perhaps.

"Were you wearing the amulet at the time?" Shay bounced the sonic grenade in her hand.

James nodded. "Yeah. He was a level four. Nasty piece of work. Later got blown up by some other asshole when he was in a helicopter, so I figured that was my revenge."

"Let's see it how it goes." Shay pulled something that

looked like heavy duty headphones over her ears, then pressed the button and tossed the grenade.

James gritted his teeth as the skin of the grenade slid back and a high-pitched whine filled the air. The grenade clattered against the floor, leaving his ears ringing but nothing more. No nausea, no rebellious stomach.

Shay pulled off the headphone looking things and tossed them on a shelf. "You okay?" She tilted her head to the side, curiosity on her face.

James nodded and shrugged. "Yeah. Barely felt it."

"That's very interesting." Shay lowered her gaze and stared directly at his chest. "That means that whatever the Whispering Amulet of Doom is doing, it's not just hardening your skin."

"When I put it on, it hurts like hell. It's like it's going everywhere in my body."

The amulet whispered low and sporadically in his mind.

Shay ran her tongue inside her cheek, her brow furrowed in deep thought. "Wonder if it'd work against mental attacks?"

James grunted. "Don't know. The despair bug got into my head, but it's not like I run into that kind of crap a lot."

"Good thing, then."

Shay moved to the last table, which contained a wooden rack holding stoppered bottles. "Time for acids and a few other nasties." She grinned.

"Remember, I don't have a healing potion. Don't hurt me too badly."

"Oh, I'll keep that in mind. Maybe." Shay winked.

*Gonna be a long afternoon.*

4

R oyce eyed the bounty hunters and trainees as they completed another set of fifty burpees. At this point, most of the men might have had stood a good chance of making it through Marine Corps Recruit Training.

*Maybe James could spare a few of these guys for the Corps.*

He chuckled and shook his head. Once a Marine always a Marine.

"Forty-eight…forty-nine…fifty," he called off as he completed each motion of the exercise. "And stop."

The assembled men grumbled. Several wiped sweat from their heads, but at least none of them fell or vomited. When he'd started training them, several of them couldn't handle one solid session of PT. Their tough gang lifestyles might have instilled bravery in them, but it hadn't given them shit in terms of discipline or endurance. Trey was one of the few who hadn't needed to be completely remade.

*A gang member might be ready to do violence, but he's not a warrior. Trey's got a warrior spirit, which was probably why he was leading these guys.*

"The team heading to Vegas should go clean up. Trey texted me earlier to say he was on his way. That means you, Manuel, Travis, Deshawn, Carl, and Shorty. Trey and Charlyce don't need to smell your stinky asses for the entire trip."

The men laughed and broke formation to head inside and get changed.

Royce lingered outside the building double-checking his messages. A couple of minutes passed before a huge new-model black Ford Expedition rolled into the Brownstone Building's parking lot. The drill instructor marched over toward the vehicle.

The SUV's window rolled down to reveal a frowning Trey.

"Problem?" Royce called.

Trey shook his head. "Nah, no problem. Just don't like the fact that I can't use my truck."

"Even in your big-ass truck there isn't enough room for a full team and equipment."

"But the F-350 is fucking *badass.*"

Royce resisted a chuckle. Trey might have purchased the truck to emulate his hero, but he didn't need the vehicle to live up to Brownstone. The more he operated without the truck, the more he'd internalize that truth.

"You're catching bounties, not starring in some reboot of the *Fast and Furious.*" He nodded at the SUV. "This is pretty good as far as civilian vehicles go. Doubt even Brownstone would want you rolling around in an APC or something. Now *that* would be badass."

Trey laughed. "Brownstone Agency rolling around with military vehicles. That'd show the bastards."

A blue Currus came up the street.

"Looks like your aunt is here. Be careful with this new batch."

Trey waved a hand. "It'll be all right. Even if the other fools can't catch a cold, I've still got Shorty."

"I don't have any problems with any of the men, but one thing you learn in the Corps early on is that training can help, but some men can't handle it when push comes to shove."

Trey's smile vanished. "Yeah, I get that, but these ain't just some random bitches off the street, you know what I'm saying? They've all been hardened, and they've all seen action. Now, don't get me wrong, Staff Sergeant. You've given them discipline and knowledge and wisdom and all that shit. They're better than they were before, but I know none of them bitches will break and run in a fight."

"Sometimes it's not about that. Sometimes it's about a man knowing when *not* to fire or start a fight."

"Yeah, I hear you. I'll keep that in mind."

The Currus pulled into the parking lot, and Royce resisted a frown. His time in the service had left him with a bad taste for autonomous machines. The military talked a good game about saving men's lives, but trusting machines overmuch had led to good Marines dying when they shouldn't have.

He didn't give a shit if the Currus included magic instead of being purely technological. A human should always be in control. Tools existed to serve humanity, and when they gave up control, it'd only hurt them in the end.

*Some genies you should keep in the damned bottle.*

"Problem, Staff Sergeant?"

"Nah. Just lost up my own ass." Royce gave Trey a nod. "Good luck, Trey, and good hunting."

———

Trey stifled a yawn as everyone scurried around the Vegas loft's kitchen helping to put up the groceries they'd just purchased.

"We got to do something about Brownstone," Shorty growled.

Trey spun on the man, his face hardening. "What the fuck are you talking about?"

"He made us look like bitches in that mud pit. I'm saying we need some sort of strategy. Not gonna beat him on strength, so we need to apply all that Marcus Aurelius-Sun Tzu-Clausewitz shit the staff sergeant's been teaching us."

Trey's muscles loosened. "Oh, yeah. We just have to take him by surprise. The big man is strong, but it's not like he weighs a ton."

"Ouch," Manuel shrieked. "What the fuck?"

*What now?*

Trey rounded on the man. Manuel was frowning at Aunt Charlyce and holding his hand. She held up a rolling pin like some enchanted blade of yore.

She nodded at a bag of chips. "You don't need to be getting into that bag, boy. I'm gonna make some food here, and I'm not cooking for an hour to hear you say you have no appetite."

"Didn't have to hit me," Manuel muttered.

Trey laughed and shook his head. He turned to leave.

*She's acting just like Nana. We're lucky she can still walk without a cane. Otherwise, she'd always be ready to beat our asses down.*

The bounty hunter made his escape to the balcony and pulled out his phone. He enjoyed the crisp Vegas night air and the bright lights of the city as he reviewed bounties.

After a few minutes, Manuel and Shorty sauntered onto the balcony.

"What are you doing out here, Trey?" Manuel asked.

"Looking up bounties."

"Why here, though?"

Trey laughed. "Because I know it's safer to be finding and catching bounties than being in a kitchen where a Garfield woman's cooking." He glanced down at his phone. "Yeah. I found a quick one we can go pick up in under an hour."

Shorty frowned. "How are we supposed to find an asshole in under an hour?"

"Because the big man has been letting me splash around cash, and now I can fucking go online and ask about low-level bitches to find out if anyone has seen them. Makes level ones easy." He pocketed his phone. "Let's go make some money before dinner."

---

Trey stepped out of the Expedition, and Shorty and Manuel jumped out after him. The rest of the team had remained at the loft with Charlyce. Two level ones weren't worth the entire team.

The men fell in behind him as he strode up the path to the front door. The ramshackle house lacked a lawn. Instead, it was covered from street to porch with small pebbles. A few small shrubs broke the rocky monotony, but their gnarled and overlapping branches suggested a lack of regular pruning. The closed blinds shielded the bounty hunter's approach, and there was no sign of cameras or drones.

Trey fluffed his suit jacket. "Rare to get street-dealer bounties. I don't know if these guys are stupid or just greedy, dealing close to schools so many times." He nodded to Manuel. "You take the back."

"You got it, Trey." The bounty hunter jogged around the side of the house.

"You want to take a shot at knocking, Shorty?"

"Damned right, I do. I don't have to be smooth and shit like you though, do I? I don't want to do this shit Trey-style."

Trey laughed. "You do what you do best, brother. We ain't all gonna have the same style."

In his years running the gang Trey had become used to micromanaging everything, but the Brownstone Agency couldn't be run the same way. His boys would need to learn to start thinking for themselves, especially if things kept growing.

Shorty glanced down at his suit. "Still not sure about this look, but whatever. I look good in whatever I wear."

Trey grinned and followed the other man to the front door. Shorty knocked loudly.

"Yo, open up. Need to chat with you."

They waited for the sounds of the back door closing or any shouts from the back of the house. Instead, after a moment the door swung open, and a huge man with a scarred face glared at them.

"Who the fuck are you supposed to be?" the man rumbled.

Shorty glanced at Trey, who nodded back.

"We're with the Brownstone Agency," Shorty explained, his low voice full of implied menace. "We're here for you and your buddy. Come along nicely, and we won't have any trouble."

The man's hand dropped to his back. Shorty and Trey whipped out their guns before the bounty had even touched the grip of his gun.

"Don't do it, bitch," Shorty growled. "You ain't worth nothing to us dead. Put your hands on your head, turn around, and get on your knees. Or die. I don't give a fuck which, but it'll mean we wasted gas money."

The bounty frowned and turned around. "Fuck you, assholes."

There was a shout from the back, and then a loud moan.

Trey nodded to the bounty. "You take care of him. I'm gonna go check on Manuel."

Shorty nodded. He already had his cuffs ready.

Trey sprinted around the corner, his gun out. A body lay on the ground, Manuel kneeling on his back.

"You okay, Manuel?"

The other man grinned. "Yeah. Don't worry, Trey, I didn't kill this bitch. I just knocked his ass out."

"Makes him easy to handle." Trey chuckled. "Let's take these asses to the 5-0 and go get some food."

---

Aunt Charlyce glared at Trey as he stepped into the room. "I thought you said you'd be right back, but it's been two hours, boy."

"I thought it'd only take an hour, but Sergeant Choi wasn't in. It was some other bi…some other cop who didn't even know how to work the damned computer. Sorry."

"Go heat up your food in the microwave. And I'm still holding you responsible, Trey."

"I'll do all the cleanup. That make up for it?"

She narrowed her eyes and looked him up and down. "For now." She stormed off.

Shorty laughed. "Next time we should just throw your aunt at the bounty."

"Nah." Trey stared down the hallway. "You don't use a nuclear weapon for low-level bounties."

---

Tyler stepped into the Seven Hills, thankful that he'd chosen a nice suit. Everything he'd heard about the Seven Hills suggested a swanky place, but you could never tell in Southern California. Sometimes the most elite restaurants maintained a casual atmosphere.

*At least this place also has a reputation for being discreet and exclusive. It might be a nice place to do high-end business, but I'd need some serious customers to justify the prices.*

He stepped up to the maître d' and cleared his throat. "I'm here with Lieutenant Maria Hall."

The plastic-looking maître d' gave him a cool smile and motioned behind him. "Right this way, sir."

Tyler fell in behind the man as they stepped into the darkened main dining room. Light chatter filled the room along with the faintest hint of classical music.

As he was led to a table he spotted a familiar face, the starring actress from the *Oriceran Dark Avenger* franchise and her long-time but allegedly currently ex-boyfriend.

*Huh. From what I heard they were supposed to hate each other. I would have put money on it.*

"Your table, sir."

Tyler tried to not let his jaw drop. Maria sat at the table. Her dark hair was up, and instead of the loose uniform, she wore a low-cut and high-slit black evening gown. He slipped into the chair across from her, swallowing.

Makeup, skin and toned body on display, and even sweet perfume. The tough AET lieutenant had been transformed from a cop into a woman. For the first time since meeting Hall, she kindled the flames of desire in Tyler.

Maria snapped her fingers in front of him. "Hey, you there?"

Tyler blinked and shook his head. The maître d' had long since wandered off.

"Uh, sorry. Just got distracted." Another quick check of the room revealed several famous actors and musicians, and a few local politicians.

*There's no way I could ever get into this place without an invitation.*

"I just wanted to give you a little thank you for your

help with everything," Maria explained. "Even if I've changed my mind about a lot of stuff, that doesn't mean I've forgotten how you helped hook me up with Dannec. I don't know if I'd be alive today without that. You saved my life, and those of my men."

Tyler took a sip of wine, some of the tension dissipating. Chatting over food and booze, he could handle.

"Well, I'm earning money, so I'm benefiting from it. Not to mention you're helping enforce neutrality."

Maria traced the rim of her glass with her finger. "Yeah, you were running a business before I ever showed up. You could have told me to fuck off. I know how you feel about cops."

"Maybe, but this is a nice place. Probably nicest I've been in a while."

Maria picked up her glass and took a sip. "Good to relax. I forget that a lot. The world's always going to spin on, and there will always be new scumbags. It's hard to not obsess over them."

"Can't worry about that. I mean, it's not like you're going to solve all crimes. All you can do is protect people."

"I guess you're right."

Tyler took a sip of wine. The arrival of the antipasto cut off more responses. They both spent some time sampling meats and cheeses before Tyler spoke again.

"You look good, by the way," Tyler commented. "Haven't seen you looking like that before. Took me by surprise."

Maria laughed. "Like an actual woman?"

"Just saying I'm used to seeing you in a uniform, not a dress."

"You're not looking so bad yourself. I mean, your little bartending outfit is nice, but you fill out a suit well."

Tyler raised a glass. "I try to please."

His gaze cut to the side. A too-young busty blonde was draped over a local alderman. A *married* local alderman who was rather famous for his commitment to family values.

*I could use that. Wait. No, I shouldn't. This place is like the Black Sun. Anything that happens in here is off-limits. Might be nice to know, but I'm not going to screw things up by using it. Instead, I'm going to concentrate on the woman in that killer dress in front of me.*

Tyler smiled. "I appreciate the invitation, Maria, and I'm glad your recent opinion changes didn't involve deciding I was a scumbag."

Maria grinned, her eyes twinkling with amusement. "The night's still young." She raised her glass. "How about a toast to befriending people you least expect?"

Tyler raised his glass. "To befriending people we least expect."

They clinked their glasses.

*Still not sure if this is a date, but I'm glad I came.*

5

The next evening, Tyler polished glasses and hummed. The Black Sun might not be the Seven Hills, but he owned it, and it was a far classier joint than it used to be.

"Someone's in a good mood," Kathy commented with a grin.

"What? Am I not allowed to be in a good mood?"

She shrugged. "Just wondering if something good happened."

"Nothing happened. I just had a nice night."

Kathy tilted her head, her eyes narrowing. "Yeah, that sounds about right. You should enjoy it while it lasts, though."

Tyler frowned. "What do you mean?"

"Just saying that Brownstone might be quiet, but he's going to get his revenge on you for that stunt with the women sooner rather than later. This is a guy who basically wasted an entire gang for killing his dog, after all."

Tyler groaned and slumped against the bar. "Shit.

You're right. I keep letting it slip my mind, but that bastard already doesn't like me. There's no way he'll let this go." He scrubbed a hand over his face. "What if he wrecks my place? Even if I could afford it, I can't have a decent business if we're undergoing a bunch of construction."

"I doubt he'll do anything too direct. He doesn't want to piss off the cops."

"He doesn't have to do anything directly. He could pull bullshit like he did last time, send high-level criminals at me and then tell the cops they are there and hope for trouble. It's not like Maria can guarantee every cop will leave this place alone."

Kathy eyed him with a faint smirk. "I'm sure *Maria* can do a lot more than you expect."

Tyler glared at her. He didn't have the time or desire to deal with the other bartender messing with him. Right now he had a huge target painted on his back, and he needed to figure out the best strategy to protect himself from Brownstone.

"Maybe the best defense is a good offense."

Kathy crossed her arms over her chest. "I'm not following you."

"Maybe if I hit him with another prank, that'll convince him not to hit me back."

"I doubt that."

A customer at the bar chuckled. "I agree with Kathy. You hit him again, the man's not gonna walk away. He's gonna come back twice as hard. He's fucking James Brownstone, not some punk kid from middle school."

Tyler rubbed his chin. "But maybe I could prove to him that I'm not worth messing with?"

"How?"

"That truck of his. Maybe I do something to his truck."

Kathy grimaced, and everyone sitting at the bar shook their heads.

"I've heard the only thing Brownstone loved more than his dog is that truck," Kathy commented. "You fuck with that truck, he might very well come and blow up this bar."

Tyler scrubbed a hand over his face. "Then maybe I give up on offense and go back on defense."

"How?" asked another customer.

"You know, have people follow him around. Watch him or some shit."

"That'll just piss him off. He'll think you're trying to fuck with him."

The first customer gulped down some of his rum and Coke and set the glass down. "You know, you could just apologize to him."

Tyler stared at the man like he'd opened a portal to Oriceran right there in the Black Sun. "What?"

"You know, tell Brownstone you're sorry."

"Fuck *that*. I'm not apologizing to that asshole. This was revenge for something he already did to me."

"Maybe you'll get lucky, and he'll let bygones be bygones."

Kathy snickered.

Tyler shook his head. "I can't plan on that. No, that fucker's got something up his sleeve. He's just waiting for me to let my guard down before he comes at me." He stared at the front door. "He'll come. I just need to be ready."

*You won't win this time, Brownstone. Not against me.*

A couple of hours passed, and Tyler's thoughts had gone from paranoia back to his favorite subject: money.

Brownstone would come for him. That much was certain, but there had to be some way to make money off it. Maybe he could start a pool for when Brownstone would get his revenge, with bets about the exact type of revenge, the monetary value of the damage, and that sort of thing?

*I've made a shitload of money betting on Brownstone. I know I could make money off this. Or shit, for that matter, maybe money off something other than when assassins are going to take his ass down.*

Maria pushed into the Black Sun. She was still in uniform, much to Tyler's disappointment. After seeing her in a dress, he couldn't help but wonder what it'd be like to see her without any clothes.

*Yeah, right. Not like a cop and a crook are ever going to get together, even for a one-night stand. And she's on Team Brownstone now. She'll probably start hating me soon.*

The AET officer marched up to the bar.

*Then again, in the meantime, she might be helpful in a different way.*

"Hey, Maria." Tyler nodded toward the hallway. "Wanted to chat with you about something in private."

She shrugged. "Okay, but I hope it won't take too long, because I could really use a drink."

"It won't take long. After that, you can have whatever you want on the house."

Maria grinned. "Free's a great price."

A quick trip brought them to Tyler's office. Once he sat behind his desk, he spoke. "I was wondering if I could ask you a few questions off the record."

"Maybe. Remember, just because we have a few deals going doesn't mean I'm going to leak a bunch of cop shit to you."

Tyler waved a hand. "Nothing like that. If anything, I'm more interested in information that hasn't even got any current value."

"What are you playing at?"

He leaned forward with an eager gleam in his eye. "The Drow. I mean, unlike your last takedown there weren't a zillion news choppers around, and your official statements have been pretty lacking in detail."

She shrugged. "This is one of those diplomatic messes. The mayor and the chief want to keep that shit as quiet as possible. It's one thing if it's some Earth witch causing a mess, but if we make too much noise about Oricerans causing trouble, it'll raise tensions or some shit. That's the message I'm getting."

"It wouldn't hurt to tell me a little. As you pointed out the other night at dinner, without my help the AET might have been up Shit Creek the last few fights."

Maria snorted. "That's how you're going to play it?"

"Just saying I'm a curious guy. I want to know a little more about the Drow and how they stacked up against everyone's favorite bounty hunter."

The cop thought about that for a few long moments, her face scrunched in concentration. "It's not like it's any big secret other than the brass wanting to keep shit quiet, and fuck Dannec knows a lot of it, so it wouldn't hurt if I passed along a little information."

"Exactly."

"Okay, then, Tyler. Ask what you want, but I'm not guaranteeing I'll answer."

He shrugged. "Fair enough. First of all, how tough were the Drow individually?"

"Easily would have been level-five bounties. Crazy shadow magic, partial flight, blades, ranged weapons, and defensive spells. Even when we got to them, the damned bastards regenerated."

"And you and Brownstone took them on at the same time?"

Maria shook her head. "They got the drop on him before we could get there. We showed up just in time to save his ass."

Tyler didn't even bother to hide the grimace. His nemesis had been *that* close to dying, only to be saved by a woman who supposedly hated him.

"So even the great James Brownstone's just a man in the end."

"Sure. A man who took on three bastards who could probably hold off an entire AET team individually, but sure." Maria shrugged. "We threw the works at them. Didn't have our drones with us, but stun rifles, bullets, anti-magic bullets, and railguns, and that included Brownstone having worn them down before we showed up. Dannec gave me a little party favor that helped."

"And that was how you won?"

Maria shook her head. "Nope. We won because of Brownstone's quick thinking."

Tyler's face twitched. "Seriously?"

"The Drow tried some super-spell. Don't even know what the point was. I think they were trying to suck out Brownstone's soul or some shit. They were ranting about it, but only Brownstone was close enough to make out most of it, and all he said was that they really wanted his ass dead."

"Guess they aren't so bad," Tyler muttered.

Maria smirked. "Anyway, they blasted him, but this artifact he had on him absorbed it, and he used it as a little magical bomb, and then the fuckers…" Her smile vanished. She leaned forward, and her expression turned icy. "If you breathe a word of what I'm about to say to anyone, this place and the neutrality are done. You understand?"

Tyler sat up, startled by the woman's sudden vehemence. "I value our working relationship, Maria. I'm not going to fuck that up."

*Plus, I want a chance at something more than a working relationship.*

She eyed him for a few seconds before nodding. "The assholes were doing some seriously messed-up magic. To be honest, I think they were about to blow all our asses to Hell, and I mean that literally. Another cop got off a lucky shot at them, but the level of magic…" She took a deep breath and slowly let it out. "These Drow could have flooded the county with demons or shit like Tessa Vansant's monsters. If it hadn't been for Brownstone's quick thinking, I'd probably have gotten torn apart by some fucked-up thing that my mind couldn't even imagine."

Tyler grimaced, bile rising in the back of his throat.

"Damn. That's fucking intense. I'm glad you took those assholes down."

"From what we've been told, the Drow won't be stopping by Earth again anytime soon. I don't know all the ins and outs of Oriceran politics, but the guys at the consulate were very, very pissed over all this shit."

"I can't imagine anyone working there wants demons flooding Earth any more than we do."

Maria let out a pained laugh. "Yeah, I'd hope so."

Tyler took a deep breath. This wasn't the time to be impressed with Brownstone. He needed information he could monetize somehow.

"You said you had to save Brownstone's ass? He must have been pretty torn up."

"Not as torn up as you'd think. Look, the reality is, if there'd only been two of them I think he could have won, but even one of them would have been enough to give *us* trouble. I hate to say it, but that's how tough he is." Maria shrugged. "Why the sudden interest in the Drow shit?"

"I like to know what's going on in my town. It helps me keep my eye out for troublemakers."

Maria snorted. "Like yourself?"

Tyler grinned. "Yeah, like myself."

6

James made his way to a back table at the Leanan Sídhe. Every once in a while, another patron gave him an appreciative nod.

*Fuck. Are they nodding because of my bounty hunting or because of that Bard of Filth shit?*

He couldn't be sure. It felt like everyone had looked at him differently ever since his delivery of dirty limericks, but it might all be in his head.

The amulet whispered something. He didn't understand it, but he could perceive the irritation. Maybe the amulet was a prude.

*Fuck you. I had to do it. I owed the Professor.*

The bounty hunter muttered to himself as he dropped into a chair across from the Professor. James frowned as he looked up at the other man. The Professor stared back at James, his face serious and no scarlet dotting his cheeks. There wasn't even a glass or mug of beer in front of him.

A chill ran up James' spine. A stone-cold sober Smite-Williams was damned unnatural.

"Good evening, lad. Thanks for coming on such short notice."

James shrugged. "Got nothing else going on, especially since Shay's out of town doing shit for you."

The Professor managed a weak smile. "Oh, she's just in the Midwest, not far away at all. She's collecting a little something for me there that ended up in some Native American burial grounds that doesn't belong there. I'm sure she'll be back soon. It's not like she's off in the middle of the Australian Outback."

"Yeah, there's that, but you called me here, not Shay." James leaned forward. "This better not be about picking up another Clown of Doom from a pawn shop."

"No, lad. I only wish it were so straightforward."

"*Straightforward*? That clown almost blew me up."

The Professor wagged a finger. "From what you told me that artifact saved your life, and probably the lives of those AET officers."

James grunted.

The Professor chuckled. "But we're not here to talk about the past. We're here to talk about the future, and the artifact you're going to recover for me."

"Why me? This sounds like Shay shit, and you said she'd be back soon."

"The lovely Miz Carson is an excellent tomb raider, but this job might require a more direct and less archaeological approach."

"Straight ass-kicking?"

The Professor shrugged. "That's one way to refer to it."

"What's going on, exactly?"

"I acquired a golden plaque. The artifact is useless on its

own, but it does have some use when combined with other artifacts, including a vimana."

James furrowed his brow. "Isn't a vimana some sort of ancient flying machine?"

"In this case think more flying castle, but yes."

"And this plaque is important to that?"

The Professor nodded. "It's a sort of navigational program. The problem is, I may have made an inelegant choice of whom to trust in this matter."

"What the fuck does that mean?"

"It means that the plaque should have been delivered to me by one Warren Sanderson yesterday but it wasn't, and Mr. Sanderson has been conveniently avoiding responding to my various communication."

James shook his head. "Wait, you telling me that you think this guy you hired took your plaque and ran?"

"It's a strong possibility. I was going to have my associate Correk look into it, but he's not available. Not only that, but this is my screw-up, so I need to eat the cost of cleaning it up." He pointed at James. "You have a good nose for hunting people down and applying just the right level of violence." The Professor held up a hand. "Right now I'm interested only in your availability. I still have a few last channels of communications I'm checking into before giving up on Mr. Sanderson."

"Alison's coming home soon. It's not like I can trek around the world looking for some douchebag artifact thief."

"Oh, it won't be like that. It'll be a local matter, and I should know very soon—within a day or so—if I need your services."

James shrugged. "Okay, then I guess I'm open. What are we talking about pay-wise?"

The Professor grinned. "I could give you money, but you do not exactly lack that, and it doesn't motivate you nearly as much as the lovely Miz Carson. How about something better?"

"What's better than money?"

"I'll owe you a favor, and when you come for it, this time I won't be able to make you participate in a dirty limerick competition."

James grunted. "I might win next time."

"But do you *want* to participate again?"

The bounty hunter grimaced. "Nope."

"We both know, lad, that you're going to end up needing an artifact or two in the future. This will just facilitate the process."

*Why do I have a bad feeling about all of this?*

"It's not like you to get taken," James observed.

"Aye, that's true, but we all make mistakes now and again."

James shrugged. "Okay, I'll stick around town the next couple of days."

The Professor smiled, but James' stomach tightened. Something about the whole thing smelled off.

It wasn't that he didn't trust the Professor. The man had been honest with him for years. It took a few seconds and a hint of derision from the amulet until James realized what was bothering him.

*This is the first major mistake the Professor's made in a long time, which means this Sanderson asshole isn't some lucky small-timer. This shit might be tough.*

The amulet's eagerness was hard to ignore.

*What are you gonna do if I end up dead, asshole?*

---

"Quiet night, Maria?" Tyler asked from behind the bar.

The woman laughed. "Yeah, quiet night. Between the Drow and Tessa Vansant things have been tense lately, so it's nice that LA is sticking to the old-fashioned kind of assault and murder that doesn't need an AET team."

Tyler poured her a drink and set it in front of her, hoping his eagerness wasn't showing. A night of careful thinking had finally produced a useful idea on how to make some more money off Brownstone, but since Maria had joined Team Brownstone, he needed to be careful how he probed the issue. Not only that, but his plan might also require a little help from AET.

"That armor you wear on the job is pretty badass," he began.

Maria shrugged. "It's useful and light-weight, but damn it doesn't exactly breathe. Let's just say I'm glad I'm not on an AET team in Phoenix."

"But it's got all those cool features. Radio…fuck, it has a built-in camera, too, right?"

"Sure, but that's not all that impressive. Pretty much every LAPD officer has a body cam. We just have a headcam instead."

*Perfect. That means a shitload of different guys getting video of every incident from different angles. It's like having a whole film crew there.*

"I was thinking the other day about what you said about

Brownstone," Tyler continued. "And how that Drow shit went down way out of town."

Maria sipped her drink. "Yeah, what about it?"

"Well, because of that you all could really let loose, right? You didn't have to worry about blowing up some poor sonofabitch's car or hurting some innocent person in the crossfire."

"Yeah, it was a good location. Wish we could have had explosive drones with us, but it was still a good place for a showdown."

"So there's a lot of value in level fives getting taken down outside of town?"

Maria nodded. "Yeah. Innocent people don't get hurt, and property damage is minimized. That makes the mayor happy, which means the chief is happy, and that means no one is screaming at me."

*It also means that no one else, including the news, has a chance to record shit. That Drow battle would have been epic to witness. How much would people pay to see something like that?*

"Kind of was thinking about that the other day; what I could do to help," Tyler commented.

Maria set her drink down, disbelief coloring her face. "Help?"

"Look, I'm an info broker, not some sort of sadistic douchebag, and I don't like level-five psychos rampaging through the city. Sometimes I hear things, and I might be able to let a certain asshole bounty hunter know. Maybe I could even whisper some things to the right ears, so his bounty ends up at a convenient location outside of town."

"If you know about level fives, you should just tell AET."

The plan was almost foolproof. He could hype a fight online and then push Brownstone and a bounty together. The trick would be getting AET there in time to get video without them spoiling the whole thing. Once they had video, he could easily get his hands on it by throwing a little cash around. A little creative editing plus internet hype, and he'd be a fight promoter.

It wasn't like he was doing anything wrong. Level fives needed to be taken down anyway. All Tyler was doing was working an angle that'd earn him a little extra money in the process.

Tyler nodded. "Yeah, sure, but I figure since you're on Team Brownstone now, you wouldn't mind him taking a whack."

Maria arched a brow. "I'm not on his team. I'm just not obsessed with blaming him for everything."

*This is working great. She's not coming to the conclusion that I have an idiot stick up my ass.*

"Just saying." Tyler shrugged. "It was something I was thinking about."

"If you can steer the next asshole away from a population center, then yeah, go ahead and do it. What's your angle here? You looking for a finder's fee from Brownstone?"

"I was thinking more like some sort of informant fee from AET."

Maria snorted. "So much for the goodness of your heart, huh?"

"Hey, if I can profit and help you take down a scumbag, isn't it a good deal for everyone?"

"I'm sure we can figure something out. It probably won't be a lot, though. Don't get your hopes up."

*Oh, don't worry, Maria. The money from the video and gambling will more than make up for it. I just don't want to leave any money on the table.*

Tyler shrugged and shot her an innocent smile. "I'll live. Not every day can be a big payday."

*Need to get Brownstone over here and see if I can work some angles on him.*

---

7

Tyler paced back and forth behind the bar, Kathy eyeing him like he'd lost his mind.

"Stop it," the brunette barked.

"Huh?" Tyler stared at her.

"You're freaking me out, and you're making people nervous." She gestured toward the bar and then around the room. "And this place has too many sketchy people. You look like you're waiting for the cops to show up and haul us all off."

"It's just…fucking Brownstone."

Kathy rolled her eyes. "Look, he'll get you when he gets you. No use worrying about it now."

"No, it's not that. It's something else."

"What?"

"Every time I bet on him, I win." Tyler threw up his hands.

Kathy side-eyed him. "And that's a bad thing because?"

"Because I keep winning."

"Money."

"Yes, money."

"You're bitching about winning money?"

Tyler nodded. "Off Brownstone."

"But you *like* money."

"But I hate him, and now I'm about to try and make even more money off him. That's fucked up."

Kathy laughed. "So what? It's not like normal people love every single company they invest in. You've got to get this Brownstone rivalry thing out of your head. Stop thinking about him as some bounty hunter nemesis and start thinking about him as an investment opportunity."

"An investment opportunity," Tyler echoed. "I like that. Yeah. That will work. Time to make some more fucking money off that asshole."

---

Thirty minutes later Tyler sat at his desk and stared at his phone, Kathy's advice swallowed with a combination of irritation and doubt.

*This is a terrible idea. This is the worst fucking idea I've ever had. But then again, it could make a ton of money, and I need Brownstone to make that money. If I get lucky, maybe I lose a little bit of money, but he goes away.*

*Shit. If he goes away, I lose any chance to make more money off him.*

The information broker groaned and slumped back in his chair. Every time he'd bet on Brownstone he'd made money. It was like the universe was mocking him by forcing him to believe in a man he hated.

But hate didn't pay the bills, and he trusted his profit instincts.

He texted the bounty hunter.

**Hey, Brownstone, I wanted to talk to you later at the Black Sun about a possible business opportunity.**

Maybe the man wouldn't immediately respond, and he'd have time to relax.

No such luck. The phone chimed only a few seconds later. "Sonofabitch."

**What fucking business opportunity could you possibly have for me?**

**This isn't something I can discuss in a text message, but it's something we can both benefit from.**

**How do I know this isn't another trick? You tried to screw me over before.**

**That wasn't screwing you over. It was just a joke. Get a sense of humor, Brownstone.**

**I have a fucking sense of humor. I almost won a contest.**

Tyler blinked and stared at the text, wondering when Brownstone had been in any sort of comedy contest. He shook his head and tapped another message into the phone.

**I swear this isn't about screwing you over. This isn't about jokes. This is about the most important thing in my life.**

**What's that?**

**Money, of course.**

A minute ticked by before the bounty hunter finally responded.

**Fine. I'll consider it and come by the Black Sun later. Try anything and you'll regret it.**

Tyler didn't bother to respond. All he needed was for Brownstone to show up. Once he pitched his plan, even the arrogant bounty hunter would have to agree.

*He acts all high and mighty, but he was more than ready to bet when he knew it could make him money.*

---

James opened the door to his F-350 and stepped inside. He'd received a text telling him to stop by and chat with the Professor about the job. The thought of a little righteous ass-kicking would help him work out some of the tension suffusing his muscles after his little exchange with Tyler.

*Fucker probably has some new betting pool he wants to set up. Always trying to profit off assholes killing me.*

His phone rang and he yanked it up, not bothering with speakerphone since he was still in his garage.

Blocked number.

"Oh, now that?" he muttered. "Who is this?" he demanded.

"Heather."

"Oh," James replied, his tone softening. "You find something?"

"Yes and no."

"What the fuck does that mean?"

"Right now, it doesn't seem like there's a single source of video. It's multiple people recording Parkour Penny."

"'Parkour Penny?'"

"That's what they're calling her online. That way everyone can quickly track down the new videos."

James chuckled. Shay would hate being called "Parkour Penny."

"And you're sure it's not the same person recording the videos?"

"Yes," Heather replied. "If it's not, someone's gone to a lot of trouble to fake it otherwise. Different cameras, different encodings, different background voices. I'm thinking people might be looking for her to record things. It doesn't smell like a conspiracy or some organization if that's what you're worried about."

James grunted. He was more worried about the cops than conspiracy, but Heather didn't need to know all his business.

"Is there any way you can set it up so I know when a new video comes out?"

"Sure. That's easy."

"I mean, so they can't easily connect you and me."

Heather scoffed. "Don't insult me, Mr. Brownstone. I've got a bunch of different ways to do that, including having your phone text you through the web."

"Okay, good."

Heather snickered. "I'd say I'm great, but sure, good will do."

A text popped up with only a number.

"Did you just send me a text, Heather?"

"Yep. That's my fee."

James looked it over. Higher than he wanted, but lower than he'd feared.

"I'll transfer the money right away."

"Then I'll get to setting up your Parkour Penny alerts."

---

By the time James sat down in front of the Professor the other man had already downed several beers. Familiar rosy cheeks decorated his face, along with a smile.

"It turns out I blamed the wrong man," the Professor explained.

"Oh? You get your plaque back?"

The Professor shook his head. "No. I still need your help in recovering something from a man who is trying to sell back something that is mine. Yes, the plaque."

James frowned. "Okay, I'm confused. You said this Sanderson guy was supposed to deliver it to you."

"Sanderson can't because he no longer has the item, and it's my damned fault."

"Now I'm even more lost than before."

The Professor gulped down some more beer and let out a sigh. "I allowed something to happen that should never have happened."

"Maybe if you showed me or something I could understand better."

The older man pulled out his phone and flipped it around so James could better see the screen. "Sanderson doesn't have it anymore because he gave it to a courier to deliver to me." He tapped the phone and a video started.

A nervous-looking man in an ill-fitting suit handed a suitcase to a beautiful Asian woman with bright-green-dyed hair.

"Hey, I know her. That's Addie, the courier. She helped us before."

The Professor sighed. "Keep watching."

The nervous-looking man hurried away and Addie took a few steps, a wide grin on her face. A few seconds later, her body shimmered and a man in a white suit stood there holding the briefcase.

The Professor shook his head. "I've used her so many times that I didn't bother to ask about passphrases when I contacted her." The Professor sipped more beer. "I contacted her again yesterday and learned she'd never talked to me. I must have been talking to this man the first time."

James grunted.

"Sloppy and stupid, lad. She has procedures for a reason, and I ignored them and sent an imposter straight to Sanderson." He sighed. "He's been trying to avoid me because he realized shortly after that he'd been conned and was afraid how I'd react. But we'd both been conned."

"Shit happens." James shook his head. "Not gonna say I would have questioned her before if she hadn't made me use your dirty limerick passphrases."

"That's all in the past. The important thing is that I now have a name and address for the person trying to sell my item. The only advantage we have in this is that the thief is far too arrogant. One Gregory Schwartz is far too desperate to unload my artifact. It's made him as sloppy as I was."

"You have his address? He still in LA?"

"Yes, for now. He seems to be renting a place, and I suspect he plans to leave as soon as he makes the sale."

"Well, he's got illusion magic, or an artifact at least."

The Professor nodded. "I suspect he's got a lot more than that. I haven't had time for a deep dive into his background, but I've confirmed he's stolen artifacts from others before. He usually sells them, but we can't be certain. He might also have hired guards." He shrugged. "On the other hand, you're you. You might be able to intimidate him into surrendering."

James shrugged. "Kind of tired of dealing with people pretending to be someone else, but at least I don't have to get on a plane or spend days driving."

"Aye." The Professor smiled. "I'm hoping you can clean this mess up for me without too much trouble."

"I'll see what I can do. Any bounty on this guy?"

The Professor shook his head. "The only people who have any clue about him are people in my field. He's a very selective sort of criminal. I don't appreciate getting conned, but I suppose I can take some small solace in how selective he is." He finished his beer and grinned. "I should be honored."

James gave a feral grin. "He's gonna be very sorry he fucked with you soon. He shouldn't have decided to give you that honor."

8

"Man, I already miss our easy money," Trey grumbled.

He kept his hands tight on the wheel and rolled the SUV slowly down the street, looking for the man he'd been told could provide some information.

Shorty stared out the window. "This is shit, Trey. We can't be handling all this with just one set of wheels."

"You're right. I'll talk with the big man about getting another car or some shit."

"Also, you sure about this?" Manuel asked. "If we find the bounty we're looking for, it's gonna piss off the Mafia. Brownstone okay with that?"

Shorty and Trey snorted in unison, but the other men in the vehicle kept skeptical looks on their faces.

Manuel frowned. "It's not a stupid question."

Trey shook his head. "Nope, but I think y'all forget at times who the big man is. Motherfucker laid out the entire Harriken, all the way to Japan. We work for Brownstone now, so we don't back up from no organized crime shit.

Besides, who gives a shit if they are organized crime? We're fucking organizing bounty hunting."

"Don't be a pussy," Shorty added. "Besides, this Bruno fucker is twisted as shit. We need to get him off the streets. Fucking beating women so severely they end up in the hospital. Fucking messing their faces up on purpose."

"He don't kill them, though," Travis offered. "And they mostly hos, right?"

The man withered under Shorty's intense glare. "I don't give a shit if they hos or not. That's bullshit. Strong men don't beat down women." His hands curled into fists. "I hope Bruno Thomas tries to put up a fight. I'm gonna show him what a real beat-down is."

Trey spared him a glance but didn't say anything. The Brownstone Agency was supposed to keep it professional, but Bruno Thomas was a piece of crap. Like Shorty, Trey half-hoped he would put up a fight so they could get in a few free hits.

Shorty didn't like to talk about it, but his father had been an abusive asshole. The only reason he stopped beating Shorty's mother was that the teenager had stabbed him.

He didn't serve time because his father was too afraid to get the cops involved, but he forced Shorty out of the house. Everything ended after that. His mother left his father and moved out of state.

Trey slammed on the brakes, and everyone strained against their seatbelts.

"What the fuck?" Deshawn yelled from the back.

"It's the guy we're looking for. Come on, bitches. Let's start earning our money."

Trey threw open the door and sauntered to a tall, pale man in a trench coat lingering near a building, more an emaciated ghoul than a human being.

*Look at this fucker. He looks like a freak. No sense of style at all.*

The rest of the bounty hunters emerged from the vehicle until a half-dozen suited men loomed around the man in the trench coat.

The man looked at Trey and licked his lips. "Shit. You Jehovahs are getting a lot more in-your-face these days."

Trey chuckled. "We ain't here about God. It's more like we're looking for the devil. People tell me you're called Captain Happy?"

"Yeah, brother, I'm Captain Happy. I'll make you happy. Is that what this is about?" He pulled open his trench coat to reveal pouches lining the inside. "I got lots of shit. You like dust? I got premium dust." The drug dealer looked at the gathered bounty hunters. "I'll even give you a group discount. Don't want no one ever saying they left the Captain unhappy."

Trey shook his head. "Ain't here for drugs. Brownstone Agency don't do drugs."

"Brownstone Agency?" Captain Happy's eyes widened. "As in James Brownstone?" He swallowed.

Trey offered the man a cold grin. "The one and only. We're his boys, and we do shit for him in LA and Vegas."

The drug dealer shook his head. "This is bullshit. I don't got no bounty on me. None. I'm a criminal. I'll cop to that, but no fucking bounty. So no fucking bounty hunter should be coming at me."

Trey snorted. "Hey, now, don't piss yourself."

The bounty hunters chuckled. Deshawn, Shorty and Travis circled around to cut off Captain Happy's escape.

"We know you got no bounty," Trey continued. "We ain't here to bring you in, and as far as I know, you ain't shoving drugs down kids' throats or nothing, so we ain't even here for a free beatdown."

The drug dealer's breathing turned ragged. "Then what are you here for?"

"A little info. Fuck, we'll even pay for it. We ain't thugs. Not no more anyway."

Trey wondered if Smooth Trey would be a better persona for dealing with Captain Happy, but the problem was that the guys didn't respond well when he shifted away from the gangster speak they were used to.

"O-okay. I can give you some info. Sure, sure. Like I said, don't want anyone leaving Captain Happy saying they're unhappy." He laughed nervously.

"So a little birdie told me that you know where Bruno Thomas is hiding out." Trey braced an arm against the wall over the drug dealer's shoulder. He leaned in. "I need to fucking know where he is. 'Cause that bitch, he *does* have a bounty. Big one."

Captain Happy shook his head. "If I squeal on him he'll kill me."

Shorty grunted. "Maybe he won't get the chance if you don't."

"Come on. He's Connected, you know. Even if you get him, they might come for me."

Trey leaned in to whisper, "We're not leaving Vegas without Bruno. I don't know what my boys will do if you say no." He leaned back and grinned.

*Brownstone would beat our asses if we thugged out on someone like this bitch, but it's not like he knows about it.*

The drug dealer scrubbed a hand down his face. "Okay, okay, okay. I'm just a businessman, you know? I don't even know the fucker. I happened to see him because he's staying in this fancy house on my weekend sales route. Nice neighborhood."

Trey snorted. "You sell in a nice neighborhood?"

"Yeah, sure. At a premium. The soccer moms get off on buying their drugs from a sleazeball, you know? It's kind of a show. I really play it up."

Trey couldn't hate the man for his game—at least as long as he cooperated.

"Give me an address, and me and my boys disappear from your life like a nightmare that you forget when you wake up."

Captain Happy rattled off an address.

Trey patted the man on the shoulder. "You're all right, Captain." He pulled his wallet out, yanked out a few bills, and slapped them in the drug dealer's hand before he turned back toward the Expedition. "We got ourselves a gangster to chat with, boys."

---

Trey parked up the street from the two-story home. On their drive past, they spotted cameras and a drone. Bruno was a paranoid fuck, for sure.

"He's got a gate and a fence," Travis complained. "How we supposed to get near him?"

Trey snorted. "We climb it, bitch."

"The cops will be here in seconds if we start climbing some rich asshole's fence."

"You still thinking like a gangbanger and not like a bounty hunter. We on the side of the law now, bitch." Trey pulled his phone out of his pocket. "Brownstone warns the cops all the time about shit." He tapped in a quick text to Sergeant Choi explaining the situation and how they were about to go after Bruno Thomas.

"What if the cops show up right away? We'll lose our bounty."

Trey's phone chimed with a text from Sergeant Choi.

**Thanks for letting me know, Trey. I'll pass the info along. Even if you don't want to move on Thomas, keep him there until we can get there.**

Trey offered his best Brownstone grunt to Travis. "Shit don't work like that. You fuckers should listen when I explain this shit. The cops show up and tag Bruno, we get a reward for that, but if we already have him when the cops show up, we get the full bounty." He opened his door. "So, we're not gonna pussyfoot around coming up with complicated plans." He pressed the button on his key fob to open the back hatch. "I'm the only fucker smart enough to have a vest on. Get some vests from the back. Bruno ain't playing, and give me that small case back there."

Everyone exited the SUV and walked to the back to put on the bulletproof vests, each of which were adorned with the words 'Brownstone Agency' in stylized letters.

"When did we get *this* shit?" Shorty asked as he strapped on his vest.

"Auntie Charlyce suggested it. It's all about branding,

you know. The suits, the vests… We want fuckers to know who we are and the pain we're gonna fucking bring them."

Deshawn handed Trey the case. "What's in there?"

"Now that we've been making some money and not acting like fools, the big man has been able to get some upgrades to our licenses." He popped open the case to reveal three sonic grenades. "Which means we can use better toys." Trey pocketed one grenade. "Shorty and Manuel, you each take one. Remember, you gotta use this shit from at least ten feet away unless you want to go down too. Everyone grab a stun gun from the box in the back, too."

A couple more minutes passed until the men were armed and armored.

"Bruno's an arrogant piece of shit, so I'm not worried about him running. We're going right at him, and we'll see what he has to say." Trey nodded to the assembled men. "It'd be badass if we could all Sun Tzu Bruno into giving up without fighting and shit, but a fucker like him isn't gonna piss his pants like Captain Happy. We need his ass alive for the money, but don't be a fucking hero. Just because we're in the Brownstone Agency don't mean we're Brownstone. You know what I'm saying?"

The other bounty hunters nodded.

"Good. Let's do this shit."

Trey sauntered down the road, the other men falling in behind him in an inverted wedge formation. A few people peeked out their windows at the well-dressed bounty hunters in their vests, perhaps mistaking them for a stylish FBI team.

They arrived in front of Bruno's gate, and Trey decided

to go for the direct approach. He pushed the call button near the gate.

"Yeah?" came a rough voice over the intercom.

"Bruno Thomas. My name is Trey Garfield. You have sixty seconds to get your ass outside and into my mother-fucking cuffs. If you do that, you won't end up busted up."

A harsh laugh came over the intercom.

A few seconds later, a different rough voice responded. "Who the fuck is Trey Garfield, and why should I care?"

"I'm a bounty hunter, dipshit. As are all my boys. I don't care if you got a few friends in there."

"Bounty hunter? Listen, you piece of shit. Do you know who I am?"

Trey laughed. "Yeah, bitch. If I didn't know who you were, why would we be here?"

Bruno growled. "You think you can fuck with someone like me? Someone Connected?"

"Oh, big scary Mafia guy, huh? Fuck you, bitch. We're not just bounty hunters. We're bounty hunters with the Brownstone Agency. James motherfucking Brownstone ain't afraid of no pissant mobsters."

"Fuck you. *You're* not Brownstone. Come and get me, you pieces of shit. I'll fucking kill every last one of you."

Trey sighed and looked over his shoulders at his boys. "The talking plan failed. Time for the ass-kicking plan. When we get up there, Shorty will take the door. Everyone else spread out. We're gonna work this fucker's nerves. Smash the windows and shoot the door out."

Deshawn frowned. "We'll get cut up if we climb in through windows."

"We're going in the front. Just want to distract the

fucker. Everything we've heard about Bruno says he's tough, but he ain't too bright. Time to use that against him."

Trey moved away from the gate and jumped on the fence. No electric shocks or sniper blast nailed him.

*This ain't so bad.*

Soon, all the bounty hunters were over the fence.

Trey snorted. Bruno had made a huge mistake hiding out in the upscale suburban neighborhood. They had enough paranoia about crime to include fences and cameras, but not enough experience with actual threats for decent defenses.

The bounty hunters fanned out on either side of the front door.

"We got at least two bitches insides," Trey explained. "Shit can get annoying if we kill someone, especially if they don't have a bounty. So even though the asshole might be Bruno's friend, just knock his ass out. We don't have that long before 5-0 shows up."

Shorty moved to the front door. Trey held up three fingers, then two, then one. When he dropped the final finger, Shorty shot out the front lock. He spun back to the wall in time to avoid the bullets ripping through the door from the other side.

"That bitch tried to shoot me," he grumbled.

Trey laughed. "It wouldn't be fun if it was too easy." He nodded to the men on either side. They smashed the windows with their pistols and ducked. Bullets whizzed over their heads.

Shorty threw open the door and rushed inside, with Trey close behind.

Two large men in tracksuits stood at the base of the stairs, pistols in hand. Trey and Shorty leapt to either side as the men opened fire.

Trey yanked the sonic grenade out of his pocket, pressed the button, and hurled it toward the stairs.

*Damn, that was a good throw. I should have played baseball.*

The two idiots tried to run instead of jumping away. The grenade whined, and both men clutched their ears and collapsed to the ground, moaning. Their guns clattering to the hardwood floor.

Trey rushed to the stairs, his gun raised. The other four bounty hunters ran in. Deshawn and Travis jogged over to secure the men.

Shorty rushed up the stairs.

"Shorty, wait," Trey shouted.

"*Fuck* waiting. Bruno has an appointment with my fist."

"Y'all secure this floor," Trey ordered before hurrying after Shorty.

Three bedrooms with closed doors taunted them. Shorty kicked open the door of the first. No one was inside. Trey threw open the door to the second. The other man was at the third before Trey had finished with the second.

"Hold up, Shorty," Trey called. "We're doing this smart." He advanced toward the door. "You throw open the door on three. You feel me?"

Shorty nodded, his face locked in an angry mask. He was hungry for Bruno.

"Three…two…*one.*"

Shorty flung the door open, and Trey pointed his gun.

A flash of silver caught his attention. He jerked to the side as an aluminum bat knocked his pistol out of his hand.

Bruno Thomas stood beside the door with a crazed look on his face.

Trey gritted his teeth, his heart speeding up. His hand dropped to the stun gun, but Shorty burst past his boss and tackled the bounty before the mobster could bring his bat back. The weapon flew out of his hand and onto the nearby bed.

Both men fell to the floor, and Shorty delivered a few vicious punches to the criminal's face, bloodying his knuckles.

"Fuck you," Shorty shouted. "You're going down, you woman-beating piece of shit."

Bruno wrapped his hands around Shorty's throat and started squeezing. "Fuck you. Nobody brings down Bruno Thomas. Nobody."

Shorty's eyes bulged, and his punches grew weaker.

Trey snatched his gun from the ground. "Roll out of the way, Shorty. I ain't got no shot."

Bruno laughed. "Don't matter now, bounty hunters. You can take me in, but I'm killing this fuck—"

The criminal writhed and let out a loud moan. His eyes rolled into the back of his head, and his hands fell.

Shorty gasped for breath, and that was when Trey spotted the stun gun jammed into Bruno's side. The other bounty hunter rolled Bruno over and fished out his handcuffs. "Kill me? Bitch, *please*. You need to be magic and shit to even have a chance."

Trey kept his weapon trained on Bruno until the huge

man was handcuffed. "From now on, we all carry stun guns for all jobs."

Shorty smirked. "It was fun shocking his ass, for sure."

Bruno groaned, and a stain spread on the front of his pants.

Trey chuckled. "Guess I was wrong. He *did* piss his pants."

---

James frowned as he followed Tyler into his office. The information broker claimed he had something that could benefit them both, and the bounty hunter figured it wouldn't hurt to stop by and see what the snake had to say.

He still didn't trust the asshole, especially after that bullshit with Tyler throwing women at him, but the man hadn't steered James wrong by sending him to Anna Forsythe. The prick could be annoying, but he could also be useful, and James hoped this would be one of those times.

Tyler settled into his chair behind his desk, a fake smile plastered on his face.

James remained standing, arms crossed.

*Surprised he doesn't have more groupies around to ambush me.*

The amulet's whispers had an air of boredom.

*Hey, my job isn't all ass-kicking 24/7. Get used to it or shut the fuck up.*

Tyler folded his hands in front of him. "I don't like you, Brownstone. I've made that very clear. But just because I don't like you doesn't mean I refuse to acknowledge your skills."

James grunted. "Thanks. Not like I give a shit."

"You're as charming as usual. Anyway, the point is, some of the recent shit with Tessa Vansant and those Drow got me to thinking about the safety of Los Angeles."

"What, you suddenly give a fuck?"

Tyler shrugged. "I have an interest in my city not being blown up by psychotic magical assholes, same as you." He leaned back. "So I've decided to change my policy."

"What policy?"

"I told you before that anyone above level three had earned my respect and my silence, and I stick by that. I can't tell you where bounties are."

James frowned. "You called me here to jerk my chain?"

The amulet whispered something dark and angry.

Tyler held up a hand. "Get some fucking patience, Brownstone. Like I said, I can't tell *you* where bounties are, but there's nothing wrong with me maybe telling them where *you* are, and if you happen to know they're coming and you're in a nice, safe place away from innocent people? Well, everyone wins, right? You get to take down a crim-inal without worrying about anyone getting hurt."

James snorted. "You just want to send criminals after me."

"No, no, no. I'd do this on a case-by-case basis, and only with your permission. You'd feed me the info I'd give them, so it'd all be completely under your control."

"You're not this fucking generous. What's your angle?"

"I don't have an angle. I just care about the safe—"

"What's your fucking angle?" James bellowed, the

grinding quality of his bass voice even more pronounced than usual. "I'm not agreeing to jack shit until you tell me the truth."

Tyler let out a long sigh and shrugged. "Okay, you got me. I was thinking I could record some of this shit. Before I was thinking about maybe getting AET on site for recording, but that might not be necessary if you're picking the site. You could set up cameras. We record it and I sell it, you know, like pay-per-view. Basically, kind of like a fight promoter."

"You're fucking kidding me."

"Hear me out, Brownstone. You're a bounty hunter. You take down bounties. I'm not suggesting you do anything different than you normally do. The only difference is that it'd be easier because you'll know where and when. I don't want Drow fucks or demon witches busting up LA any more than you do. It's just I want a slice of the action. Not too much to ask, you know?"

James' expression softened, and he scratched his eyelid. "If I do this, I'm getting a cut from the video profits, too."

"Sure, sure. The fighter always gets paid. I've got no problem with that."

James uncrossed his arms and settled into the chair. Even he had to admit that Tyler had a point. If he were going to be taking down bounties anyway, there was no reason not to earn a little extra money off it. The orphanage could always use more funding.

The bounty hunter frowned. "You sure you'll even be able to get anyone? It's not like everyone is gonna show up and ask you for information."

"Sure, not everyone, but this place has a reputation as

neutral ground now so I get a lot of people showing up who might not otherwise. It's a simple matter of recognizing them and whispering the right thing."

"But won't they catch on?"

"To what? Brownstone kicking their asses? You've got a reputation for that already." Tyler furrowed his brow. "We can't always use the same location, though. Then they *would* catch on."

"Sure, but I'd like the first fight…bounty to be in the Salton Sea area. It's annoying and dry there, but it's also safe as fuck. Hell, even the AET will be happy because I'm not busting shit up."

Tyler chuckled. "Yeah, Maria's a fan now with you allegedly saving the world and all."

"I wasn't saving the world. I was saving my ass."

"Whatever. I think we've got a good plan. The Salton Sea, just need a four or higher. I'll get some cameras so simple even you can set them up. The only problem with the Salton Sea is that if you're that far out we won't be able to get AET to you quick enough for video, so you'll have to set everything up for filming. You can at least get a drone flying, right?"

James grunted. "I'm not a fucking moron, Tyler."

"Sorry. Was just asking." Tyler grinned. "Nah, this is going be great, Brownstone. We'll make a shitload of money off this."

James nodded. If this were nothing more his normal bounty hunting with a little help from Tyler, what could possibly go wrong?

Trey and Shorty stepped into the narrow alley behind the club. Their latest bounty wasn't conveniently staying in a hotel or apartment. With dozens if not hundreds of people inside the nightclub, the bounty hunters couldn't charge in and risk bullets flying. Not only would innocent people get hurt, but the big man would kick their asses all the way to Mars for taking that kind of risk.

Trey's phone buzzed with a text from Deshawn.

**Yo, we got the front covered. Bitch ain't come out yet.**

Carl followed up with a text a few seconds later.

**Manuel thought he saw him coming out the side door, but it ain't him.**

"Fuck," Trey muttered. "We need something better than just phones. It's like we're a bunch of teen girls going after a bounty."

Shorty eyed him. "What do you want, then?"

"We need to go all Secret Service- or Special Forcesstyle, you know what I'm saying? If we're doing this shit in teams, we need to be able to talk when shit goes down."

Shorty shrugged. "Talk to the big man, then. Shit, you want us in these suits and all that, might as well go all the way. Motherfuckers in suits with weird earpieces are a lot scarier than what we looked like before."

Trey laughed. "You never said that before."

"Didn't think about it before. We look like we're from the government and shit. What's freakier than that?"

Trey tugged on his suit jacket. "We're from the Brownstone Agency and we're here to help," he intoned in a low voice.

The back door swung open, and both men's hands slipped inside their jackets and inched toward their guns.

Two red-faced women in mini-dresses stumbled out, laughing and the bounty hunters lowered their hands. The woman giggled to each other, not even glancing Trey and Shorty's way as they headed toward the street.

Shorty whistled. "Maybe we should get their digits."

Trey snorted. "Bitch, we're on a job. Pay attention."

"Just saying they had nice asses."

"And I'm just saying that if you let tits distract you, you're gonna end up getting a bullet in your fucking head. Do you think Mr. Brownstone lets himself get distracted by that kind of shit?"

Shorty shrugged and returned his attention to the back door.

*Does make me think. Fucking women is one thing, but maybe I should be looking for something permanent. Now that I got a stable career and shit.*

The back door flew open again, and a lanky bald man in

a green leisure suit strolled out. It was their target, Jacob Johns.

"Got you, you son of a bitch," Trey murmured. "Get ready to move, Shorty."

A pale short-haired woman in a suit emerged right after. Despite her beautiful face, bright red lipstick, and striking red hair, Trey was more impressed with her suit. A layered combination of femininity and danger oozed from the woman.

Suit Chick's ankle-high boots clacked against the asphalt as she walked into the alley. She stopped, turning her head toward Trey and Shorty.

"Shit, that's Armani." Trey sighed. "That's way nicer than my suit. That just ain't fair."

Johns stopped and looked their way, scowling. "Who the fuck are you, the IRS?"

"Brownstone Agency," Shorty announced. "Jacob Johns, we're here to collect on your level-three bounty. Turn around and be a nice boy and we won't have to get rough."

Johns snorted. "You're not Brownstone. Why the fuck should I care?" He waved his hand dismissively. "Victoria, take care of them." He leaned against the wall and crossed his arms.

Trey glared at him. *Talk about a cocky son of a bitch.*

The woman stepped in front of the bounty, and her hand drifted inside her suit jacket.

Trey and Shorty both yanked out their guns.

"We got no problem with you," Trey offered. "So don't try nothing."

Victoria's hand stopped moving but remained inside her jacket. "You really work for James Brownstone?"

Shorty nodded. "Just walk away. I'm not down with hurting women."

"That's pretty nice of you, but if you're going be a bounty hunter, sometimes you'll run into dangerous women." She grinned. "Like me."

"Turn around," Trey ordered. "Put your hands behind you. We're gonna cuff you, and then we're gonna take your boss in. I don't know who you are, but if you ain't got a bounty, you ain't our business."

Johns snorted and continued to lounge against the wall. "Fucking morons."

Victoria shook her head. "Just to be clear, he's not my boss. More like a client."

"So, what, you his bodyguard?"

"Yes. For now."

Trey kept his gun trained on the woman, tension spreading through his body, and his heart rate kicking up. Every street instinct in him screamed that Victoria was way more dangerous than the level-three bounty resting against the wall without the faintest hint of giving a shit.

He nodded at Johns. "This guy's a serious fucker, you know. He and his boys were raiding medical supply trucks. Who the fuck does that?"

Johns snorted. "Hey, I sold that shit. People got what they needed eventually."

"Tell that to the kids who died, you son of a bitch."

Victoria's hand remained inside her jacket.

Johns pushed off the wall. "Spare me, you bounty-hunter piece of shit. You're no cop. You're just some trash from the street who thinks if he puts on a suit and calls himself a bounty hunter that he's better than me. You're not better than me. I'm a businessman. You're just a parasite."

"Shut your mouth, bitch," Shorty yelled.

"Keep it cool, Shorty," Trey ordered. They couldn't let Johns mess with them, especially when Victoria was ready to deliver a beat-down. A few seconds of distraction could be the difference between life and death.

The woman had a good face and a slender build judging by her suit, so she wasn't going to deliver a Brownstone-style beat-down. But it didn't take a lot of strength to pull a trigger.

Trey's phone buzzed with a text, but he ignored it. His earlier instincts had been right. They needed to invest in better communications gear. If all six of the boys were gathered in the alley, Johns and Victoria would have already surrendered.

Sun Tzu came to mind. To subdue the enemy without fighting is the acme of skill.

*Easy for you to say, bitch. You've been dead for twenty-five-hundred years.*

Johns pointed at Trey. "Kill that fucker. I don't like the way he's looking at me."

Victoria shook her head. "Not a hitman, Mr. Johns. I'm a bodyguard."

Shorty advanced toward Johns. "You don't have your gun out, woman. You can't win. Just turn around. You don't have to go down for a piece of shit like Johns."

She offered Shorty a thin smile. "What if I told you I don't even have a gun?"

He snorted. "You don't bring a knife to a gunfight."

"No, you bring a wand."

*Oh, hell no.*

Victoria muttered something in a language Trey didn't understand and her arm twisted. He pulled his trigger.

A bright flash filled the alley, and Victoria stood there grinning. Bright glyphs covered her suit, and her eyes glowed bright red. She twirled a thin golden wand in her fingers.

Trey and Shorty continued firing, but the bullets disappeared in flashes against her suit. The men both stopped after a few seconds, realizing the futility.

"Fuck," Trey muttered. "I thought this shit might happen one day, but not so soon." He lowered his gun.

Johns laughed. "Stupid pieces of shit. Fucking *kill* them already."

The witch shook her head. "No reason to." She smiled at Trey. "What's your name?"

"Trey Garfield."

"Victoria Stone." The witch bowed with an exaggerated flourish. "You can't win, Mr. Garfield. There's no point in trying."

"Having a small chance of winning ain't the same thing as not being able to win, but, yeah, you're a badass chick in a better suit. It's a shame to put bullets in either that body or that suit."

Victoria laughed. "I do like a man with a good eye."

Shorty ejected his magazine and reloaded, muttering under his breath. Trey holstered his gun.

The witch stopped twirling her wand. She pointed it to the side and made several quick movements. A pulsating glyph appeared in the air.

"This Brownstone Agency? That means you work for

James Brownstone, as in the Scourge of Harriken? The guy who took down the Red-Eyes Killer?"

"Yeah. He's the man at the head of everything."

Victoria's gaze flicked to the glyph and back to Trey. "Tell your friend to put his gun away. If he does, you can both walk away from this."

Trey nodded at Shorty. "Put it away. Just wasting bullets."

Shorty gritted his teeth and holstered his weapon.

Trey's phone buzzed again, but he continued to ignore it.

"Fucking kill them already," Johns yelled. "What am I paying you for, bitch?"

"To protect you," Victoria offered, a cold look in her eyes. "I'm doing just that, Mr. Johns. Unnecessary death doesn't help protect you."

Johns snorted. "Whatever."

"Call me a bitch again, and you'll regret it."

"I'm paying you a shitload of money, so I'll call you what I want, you stupid twat."

Victoria heaved a sigh and smiled at Trey. "One moment, Mr. Garfield." She reached into a pocket with her free hand and fished out her phone. After a few quick taps, she slipped it back into her pocket. "I've refunded your money, Mr. Johns."

The man blinked. "Huh?"

She turned toward the man, her face locked in a rigid smile. "I don't work for men who don't respect me. It's also not worth making an enemy of James Brownstone for such a small amount, especially to protect an idiot like you."

"These assholes don't work for Brownstone," Johns yelled. "They are just saying that to scare you."

Victoria pointed toward the floating glyph with a wand. "That's not what my spell's telling me."

"Fine, fine. I'll pay you twice as much."

"No. You forgot that just because I'm working for you, you're not my boss. Treat the people who work for you with respect and you'll get better results."

"I'm sorry, okay?"

"Too late," the witch spat. "I don't tolerate disrespect."

Trey chuckled. "That's why I like Mr. Brownstone. He's all about respect. You give it to him, he gives it to you."

Shorty pulled out his stun gun and edged toward Johns with a wicked grin on his face. "If you ain't working for this prick anymore we can go after him, right, ma'am?"

The witch nodded. "See, Mr. Johns? It's not that hard to be respectful."

The bounty's eyes widened and he sprinted away, his long strides giving him good distance. Shorty sprinted after him, but Trey didn't follow, instead still watching the witch.

"If we didn't work for Brownstone, would you have fireballed our asses?"

Victoria laughed. "Something like that." She twirled her wand with her fingers one last time before slipping it into a holster inside her jacket. The glyphs on her jacket vanished, as did the one in the air. "You loyal to Brownstone?"

"Yeah."

"I'm loyal to no one. It's all cost-benefit analysis to me." She nodded down the alley as Shorty tackled and stunned

Johns. "And the costs outweighed the benefits in this particular case." She gave a little wave and sauntered toward the street. "Be careful, Mr. Garfield. It's a dangerous world we live in, especially with all this magic floating around."

Entranced, Trey stared at her as she walked toward the street, her hips swaying.

*What a woman.*

"Yo, Trey," Shorty shouted from the other end of the alley. "You wanna help me with this fucker?"

"Yeah, yeah. Be right there."

Trey shook his head. He was now sure of a couple of things. Victoria Stone was hot, and the Brownstone Agency needed to be prepared for magical encounters.

*Fuck. Maybe I should have asked for her digits?*

James had the name and address, which meant he could skip the usual step of sniffing around contacts and go straight to the ass-kicking. He remained unsure if he should warn Schwartz he was coming or just barge in and demand the artifact. He rubbed his chin as he pondered the situation from his favorite new chair.

The first plan might result in the man surrendering right away, but it also might end up with him readying a pile of explosives or traps. On the other hand, the second plan could end up with a man so startled he'd blast anything that moved.

The tone of the amulet's murmurs made it clear that it preferred the second alternative.

*You do your job, and I'll do mine.*

James frowned. He needed to overwhelm the guy with something special. A quick call followed, but not to the target.

"Verify identity," replied a distorted voice.

"James Brownstone."

"What do you need, Mr. Brownstone," Heather asked, her voice now normal. "Something else come up with Parkour Penny?"

"Nah. This is different. I wanted to place a call to a guy. I know where he lives, but I wanted it to be scarier than usual."

"'Scarier than usual?'"

"Yeah. You're a hacker. You can probably hack his microwave and shit, right? Threaten a man through his microwave, that's got to make him piss his pants."

Heather laughed. "If it's connected to the net I can get to it, and almost everything's connected to the net these days."

James grunted. This was why he didn't trust electronics.

"I figure you hook me up to everything in the guy's house, and I give him a little warning. Sound doable?"

"Sure. Got an address?"

The bounty hunter offered the address.

"Give me a few minutes."

James spent the new few minutes reading about barbeque when his phone rang again with a call from a blocked number.

"This is Brownstone," he answered.

"You ready?" Heather asked.

"Yeah.

"Okay, you're on. I've got you talking through practically everything. TV, security cameras, even a drone feed and a dryer. The guy's a paranoid fuck, but he's not good enough to back up that paranoia."

The line clicked over.

"What the fuck is wrong with the TV?" mumbled a man's voice over the line.

James cleared his throat. "Gregory Schwartz, can you hear me?"

"Who the fuck is this?"

"My name is James Brownstone. I'm a bounty hunter."

"I don't know what game you're playing at, Brownstone, but I've got no bounties on me so you should fuck off. And you shouldn't mess around with people unless you know about them."

James grunted. "Look, asshole, consider this a courtesy call. You took something that doesn't belong to you. I'm going to come soon and collect it. You hand it back, and I walk away and you never have to worry about me again, but you make this difficult, you're gonna get hurt."

Schwartz laughed. That wasn't the reaction the bounty hunter had been expecting.

"Get hurt?" Schwartz yelled. "Get *hurt*? You'll invade my home with your tricks and fucking threaten me, you meathead piece of shit? I know all about you, Brownstone. You're nothing. You think you're tough. I have artifacts you can't even begin to imagine. Come at me, you stupid asshole. I'm going to shred you atom by atom, while you beg me to kill you to end the pain." A loud bang came over the line. "How fucking *dare* you threaten me? After I'm done ripping your atoms apart, maybe I should go and fucking demonstrate my power like that witch did at the farmer's market just so Smite-Williams learns to never, ever fuck with me. Come at me, Brownstone. Fucking come at me. I look forward to killing you and making your skull into a toilet."

*Yeah, this guy's not on the world's most stable list.*

The amulet continued whispering and murmuring in James' mind, obviously spoiling for a fight.

*Don't worry, you'll get your chance.*

James ended the call, and his phone rang a second later. "Yeah?"

"I listened to all that," Heather explained.

"And?"

"That guy's fucked up. Totally unhinged."

James chuckled. "Yeah, a lot of these guys are. I don't know if they start out that way, or if messing around with powerful magic does it. At least this asshole doesn't have a nickname."

"Do you think he was telling the truth about killing people after he kills you?"

"Yeah, I do. Gonna give him a little while to stew on things, then I'll just handle him. Was hoping this didn't have to get violent, but it doesn't seem like I have a choice."

Heather sighed. "Okay. Discount."

"Discount?"

"Maybe you're used to psychos threatening to rip you apart atom by atom, but that's kind of new for me. I'm going to give you a big discount and back you up when it comes time to take the guy down. That is, if you want it."

James thought it over for a few seconds. Shay used Peyton's help to great effect, but James had never worried about that kind of thing before. Always seemed too complicated. Heather just watching his back didn't seem that bad, though.

"Guess it wouldn't hurt to try once."

---

Trey and the boys sat around the table working on the casserole Aunt Charlyce had prepared. It'd been a good day. They'd bagged their target, a real scumbag, and no one had gotten hurt despite running into a witch and poor communication. The delicious food was a bonus.

"You say this witch just walked off?" Aunt Charlyce asked.

Trey nodded. "Johns was being an asshole, and she didn't like his attitude."

His aunt smirked. "See, that's the problem with men. They don't know when to shut up."

The other bounty hunters continued to stuff their faces, less interested in the day than the food.

Trey sighed. "The whole thing does make me think. We got to be careful when we hit the level threes, even if we don't know about magic."

"You should *always* be careful." Trey's aunt spooned out more of the casserole for him. "And you should eat up." She smiled, then sighed as she surveyed the table. "Good food, but always a mess after."

"Oh, yeah, that reminds me." Trey pointed at Deshawn and Carl. "You two are on cleanup tonight."

Deshawn put down his fork. "Huh? Why me?"

"Because we're all gonna take turns, except Auntie Charlyce."

"Why not her?"

"Because cooks don't clean. I suggest you learn to cook if you don't like to clean."

10

James frowned as he made his way toward his front door. He needed to make a quick trip to Zoe's place for a few more health potions. After the rant the other day it was obvious that Schwartz wasn't even close to surrendering, and he'd have to handle the situation the more traditional straightforward Brownstone ass-kicking way.

*I knew I should have just barged in. Could have taken the fucker completely by surprise.*

His phone chimed with a text alert.

**AUTOMATED ALERT: Two new videos for Parkour Penny. Links follow.**

James frowned and tapped the first link. An awful and grainy night video of someone leaping rooftops followed. Given the distance and poor quality of the recording, he couldn't even be sure it was a woman.

*This is the shit I'm worried about?*

"Here she is again," blathered a male voiceover. "The mysterious woman we've taken to calling 'Parkour Penny.'

The guy who recorded this video said he spotted her several minutes before, but he had to concentrate on keeping up with her before he could try to get some video. That's the grace and elegance of our Goddess of Movement."

James snorted. He'd describe Shay many ways, but not graceful and elegant. This was a woman who complained about assassins being pussies because they didn't get close enough to targets to get their blood on them.

Some additional banal filler followed until the end of the short video. James started the second.

*Okay, this is more of a problem.*

In the new video someone was following Parkour Penny, and even from a distance, James could recognize his dark-haired girlfriend, if only from her movements. The camera angle suggested a headcam.

Shay leapt from one building to another and the cameraman followed, but she had a couple dozen yards on him for most of the video.

*That's impressive, but it's also not shit I'm ever gonna be doing. Parkour makes even running complicated. How the fuck do you make running complicated? Guess that's the French for you.*

Another voiceover kicked in with commentary. "You have to think that a woman who can move like that has a hell of a nice body, and I love me a tight, athletic body."

James gritted his teeth.

"Yep," offered another voice. "This is an athlete with no fear. I think she'd be a hellcat in bed. Screw the fantasy of being with a gymnast. I want to be with a parkour woman."

James grunted, his hand tightening around his phone. These assholes were talking about his woman.

"I wasn't able to get close to her that night," continued the first voice, "but maybe next time."

"Shit. I think that if a man can't keep up with her, he doesn't even have the right to think about asking her out. You should just give up now."

*You assholes can't keep up with the real Shay. I'm a real man, not you.*

"Screw you," the first man responded. "I've gotten closer than almost anyone. I'm sure she's watching these videos. She'll contact me when the time is right."

*You fuckers stay away from Shay, or I'll show what it's like to sail through the air after I punt your asses.*

James snorted and then took a deep breath. What was he even worried about? It wasn't like Shay was going to leave him for some parkour asshole. She still needed to be careful about getting caught, but so far, it seemed like her issue was more groupies than cops coming after her.

*Guess she can feel a little of the bullshit I have to deal with. Maybe next time Tyler sets me up, I won't have to worry about getting rid of the video.*

James finished the video on mute and headed out the front door. He had more important things to worry about, like healing potions and kicking Gregory's Schwartz's ass.

*Fucker was probably lusting over Shay too.*

---

A long, winding road continued up the hill. After his trip to Zoe, James headed toward the address, which brought him into an unincorporated area in the San Gabriel Valley foothills. A few homes dotted the road on either side, but at least James wouldn't have to worry about innocent people being caught up in his fight with Schwartz.

*Unless the fucker opens some magic portal to another dimension.*

James scoffed. The man talked a good game, but the bounty hunter doubted Schwartz was as badass as his rant. People who were both strong and vicious didn't rely on tricks like illusions to take what they wanted. It was obvious Schwartz wanted to convince James he was a threat to scare him off, but the bounty hunter wasn't buying it.

*Yeah, he'll probably be crying by the time this is over. Maybe I should make him record an apology to the Professor?*

The amulet whispered something in James' mind. For a second, he almost thought he could understand the words. Something about enemies and strength. Even without full understanding, the amulet's desire to test itself against Schwartz was obvious.

"I've got you on long-range from my drone," Heather reported via James' earpiece. "You sure you want to use jammers? I won't be able to help you as much. I'll keep this drone flying outside jamming range, but it's too far to get good IR from the house. I'll still do my best to hit the household defenses, but Schwartz has already disabled a lot of them from what I can tell. I can't communicate with you under jamming even if I can hack his hardline stuff, but he's already killed the power in the house to disable his electronics so not much I'll be able to do."

"Don't worry about it. He *wants* me to come. Arrogant

fuck. Just keeping an eye on him has been helpful. If I need more help, I'll kill the secondary jammer once I'm inside."

"If you're sure?"

"I'm sure."

James stopped his F-350 in front of a rusty metal gate blocking the final stretch of the road. A weathered ranch house stood at the end of the road a few hundred feet up in the hills.

A huge TRESPASSERS WILL BE SHOT sign hung on the front of the gate right next to an equally large NO SOLICITING sign.

"I hope Shay's having a fun time on her tomb raid," James mumbled. "I don't think this shit's gonna be fun at all, even if it ends up being easy. Stupid Schwartz."

The bounty hunter backed the truck farther down the road. No reason to risk an RPG attack on his beloved F-350. Only luck had saved it from destruction when his house was blown up, and even that incident had been far too close for comfort.

James grabbed a go-case he'd picked up earlier from the back and fished out the last few pieces of equipment. Just because he didn't believe Schwartz would be much of a threat didn't mean he shouldn't be careful. He might be wrong. The man had artifacts.

With plenty of spare mags, multiple throwing knives, and a few more grenades than usual, James was ready to kick some ass. He might not be able to destroy an entire international gang with his loadout, but it'd work for one man, even a well-prepared one.

James pulled a few jammers out of the go-case before tossing it into the backseat.

"Jamming now."

"Talk to you later, Mr. Brownstone," Heather replied.

James activated the first jammer and set it on the passenger seat. He slapped the second on his wrist, then pulled out his phone and tossed it on the seat too. It'd be useless with the jamming anyway.

*Hope no nature lover is running their drone nearby.*

Despite the warm temperatures, he was still wearing one of his now-standard-issue Shay-disapproved shabby gray coats. It was nice to have a few extra pockets filled with gear when you were about to blow something up or kill a man or twenty.

The bounty hunter jogged up the road and activated the other jammer. He hadn't spotted any drones and neither had Heather on his drive up, but this would save him from any surprises from above, and maybe a few household defenses if Heather couldn't handle them or they were wireless access only.

He approached the gate, his gun still in his holster. With the house so far up the road, James doubted the battle was going to start until he kicked in the front door. He'd worried that Schwartz might run, but Heather's surveillance hadn't spotted any unusual movement.

James snorted. Schwartz had bragged about his artifacts, but his gate lacked useful magic like the glamour redirecting people from the School of Necessary Magic. He wasn't as big a deal as he thought.

*You're not so tough, asshole. We'll see who is crying and begging by the time this shit is over.*

The bounty hunter walked the width of the gate until he found the latch keeping it closed.

"Yeah, so much for your badass security. But I'll give you this, asshole. It's hard to hack a simple latch." James reached over to the gate to flip the latch.

A roar deafened James and flame blinded him. A few seconds passed before he realized he'd been flung into the air. Several more passed before he slammed into the ground, kicking up dirt. Dirt, rock, and bits of metal rained over the area.

He groaned and shook his head. His shabby grab coat was now only half there, but he hadn't lost any equipment. Burn marks and small bleeding cuts covered his body. There was a huge crater where the gate had once been.

The amulet's whispers picked up, hurried and accusatory.

James stood and dusted himself off. The pants, coat, and shirt were a loss, but he didn't even need a healing potion; not so bad for getting blown up.

He frowned. Heather had been watching Schwartz, which meant the man had trapped the gate before James had called him.

*What a paranoid fuck.*

"That should be the worst of it," he muttered. "That asshole thought he could blow me up at the gate, but he didn't know about the amulet." James took a few unsteady steps forward, his legs and arms aching. "Okay, good hit—I'll give him that—but he needs to finish me off to win this shit."

James frowned and stepped to the side of the road. Schwartz had probably trapped the road farther up. There was no reason to walk into his next surprise.

A few minutes passed as James proceeded toward the

house, thinking about how much fun it'd be to throw the asshole through a window.

*Fucking Schwartz. You should never have stolen from the Professor. When I get to you, I'm gonna—*

The ground gave way and James fell into sharpened metal spikes. He grunted at the sting. The trap produced a few new minor scrapes, but no serious injury unless he counted the new hole in his left boot.

*Fuck. I just bought these boots last week.*

James jumped and hoisted himself out of the pit. He stared at the pit and shook his head. If he hadn't had his amulet on he would have ended up skewered in several places. A healing potion might not have even been enough.

Again, even if he could communicate with his hacker, it wouldn't have been helpful. James laughed. Schwartz understood the power of KISS.

Something clinked in James' pocket. He frowned and checked his pouches. He'd started with three potions, but the shattered remains of one filled one of his pouches.

"Fucking Schwartz. Those things aren't cheap."

The amulet's murmurs and whispers were near-constant now. It was excited. Maybe even proud and ready to prove its power.

James stared at the pit and the road. Anything could be trapped on the way to the house, and he'd been lucky that the attacks had all been conventional. For all he knew, Heather was stopping missiles from raining down on him.

Some weird magical power lance might kill him before he had a chance to drink a potion, and even if Schwartz had been bragging about his power, the man had a history of stealing artifacts. He could have almost anything in the house.

"Main road it is. At least if I keep blowing up, it'll knock me closer to the house."

James continued up the road. He was almost to the house when he heard the click. He looked down, frowning at the portion of the road now depressed. The fake asphalt paint job seemed obvious now, not that it did him any good.

"Damn it."

He took a deep breath and jumped forward. Several loud twangs sounded, but nothing exploded. A moment later, he spotted the dark spheres hurling through the air over him.

"What the fuck?"

James leapt to the side as the spheres exploded with a hiss, releasing a cloud of greenish liquid. His quick movements spared him from the bulk of the attack. His legs stung, and new holes appeared in his pants. A few more traps and he'd be finishing this job in nothing but his socks and a tactical harness.

"Fucking acid?" He snorted. "You kidding me? Who the fuck actually makes an acid trap?"

James scrubbed a hand over his face. He ached and bled and his clothes were shredded, and he wasn't even at the house yet.

*It's like I woke up on the wrong fucking side of the bed this morning.*

11

James continued his death march toward the house. The fun had continued with a burning arrow shower and a bouncing incendiary mine. The pit filled with what he assumed were poisoned spikes had been a nice touch.

*How long has this guy been setting up traps?*

He'd made it out of the pit and to the front door without collapsing, but he wasn't sure if the amulet protected him from the poison or the poison had never made into his bloodstream. Either way, it was yet another spot where he'd have been killed without his amulet.

*Guess it's a good thing Alison browbeat me into wearing this all the time.*

It'd become easier to ignore the whispers in his mind with his recent constant use. It was almost like white noise; there but not something demanding his concentration.

James downed a healing potion. The burns, cuts, and aches on his body weren't lethal, but they'd slow him down, and he was done underestimating Schwartz. The man might be an arrogant fuck, but he also was paranoid on a level even Shay would find extreme.

The aches faded, and the wounds sealed themselves. New skin grew over the burns. He remembered halfway through to try and time the healing process, but by then it was too late to figure out anything useful.

*I've taken plenty of healing potions with the amulet on. I guess it's a good thing that it's not stopping the healing, but it doesn't seem to be making it stronger either.*

James' attention drifted to his wrist. His second jammer was missing, probably in a pit or melted to slag on the road.

He reached up. His earpiece was also gone, a victim of the traps. So much for having Heather help him inside the house.

*It was a good plan anyway. Doesn't matter. She did her part beforehand.*

James took several deep breaths and stared at the front door. He shrugged and knocked hard.

"Fucking open up, Schwartz. You've got to have seen that all your traps didn't kill me, so just give up and make this a lot easier on both of us. I'm already really pissed off here, and you don't want to piss me off more. I'm not here for your ass. I'm just here for the plaque. Give it to me, and I walk away. I don't give a fuck who you screw over after that."

*Should I kick open the door or try to get in through a window? He's going to blow me up either way. Or throw fucking acid on me. Or burn me. At least it hasn't been magic so far. Fucker.*

"Fuck it. I want this day to be over." James slammed his

boot into the door. Wood splintered, and the door flew back.

To his surprise, nothing exploded, poured acid on him, or set him on fire.

"Come out, asshole," he yelled. "This is over. You gave it your best shot, but I'm still fucking standing."

Again, no response.

*Damn you, Schwartz. You're really pissing me off, asshole.*

A backpack sat against a wall opposite the front door. The furniture had been pushed against the walls.

James stepped into the living room, frowning. He pulled out his gun.

"You arrogant piece of shit," yelled Schwartz's voice from all around him. "I don't care if you survived a few minor tricks. Now you're going to face the ultimate power. I've been thinking about it ever since your little threat. The famous James Brownstone. Once I kill you, everyone will know how powerful I am."

"Better assholes than you have tried."

"Doubtful. It doesn't matter. The end time is upon us, Brownstone. Chaos and madness. The collapse of civilization. Fools like you focus on the now instead of the future, but I've been focused on the future for years; ready, careful, and collecting what I need to survive."

"Is that what this is all about? You're some sort of survivalist nutjob?"

Schwartz scoffed. "I'm nothing of the sort. I'm a man of vision. A survivor."

James spun, his gun at the ready, seeking the man or a hint of the man. A shimmer or an unusual shadow, perhaps. Nothing. Big surprise; a paranoid asshole could hide.

"Smite-Williams crying about losing his plaque. Pathetic. I once respected him, but now I see he's weak like all of you. A fool."

"He's not the one hiding from me."

"See the backpack, Brownstone?"

James' gaze flicked to the backpack. "Yeah. What about it? Does it have a bomb or something?"

"Nothing like that. It contains the plaque. Kill me, and you can take it back to that pathetic old drunk. I won't be able to stop you, after all."

"It doesn't have to go down this way. How about I just take it and walk out of here? I'm not interested in you. I'm just interested in the artifact."

"But I'm interested in *you*." Schwartz cackled. "You think you can walk out of here after insulting me? You thought your mere name and reputation would make me beg for your forgiveness. Screw you, Brownstone. I have the power here, not you."

James grunted. "You haven't killed me yet, have you? I'm beginning to think you can't do anything but ruin my clothes and piss me off, asshole, and you've *really* pissed me off. You're lucky I'm even offering you this deal. If you're so fucking tough, then stop hiding. Pussies hide. Men show themselves."

The amulet murmured in excitement, eager for the confrontation.

Shadows pooled across the room and slid toward each other. James narrowed his eyes. The shadows flowed together and lifted from the floor, forming a white-suited man. A soft violet glow surrounded Schwartz's body, and a huge golden pendant hung around his neck.

James grunted. "Finally decided to stop hiding?"

"No. I've decided to teach you a lesson, Brownstone, about arrogance. You don't fear the future because you fear no man, and that's a mistake. I understand fear, and that gives me power."

"You are one of the more annoying fucks I've run into in a long time. I almost think I prefer King Pyro's rants to this shit."

Schwartz lifted his hands. He wore thick leather gloves covered in runes. One glove was white, the other black. "I'll make this easy for you, Brownstone. Go ahead and put on the backpack. I won't attack you until you do. Once you pick it up, I'll humble you by taking your life."

"We'll see about that." James squeezed off several shots.

Schwartz smirked as the bullets bounced off him. "A gun? Pathetic." He nodded toward the backpack. "Or you can run. I'll accept that, too. Go ahead, Brownstone. Tuck your tail between your legs and run away. I won't promise I won't kill you, but if you run fast enough, you might be able to escape with your life."

The bounty hunter holstered his pistol, flipped the man off, and walked over to the backpack. "Not impressed. Plenty of assholes are bulletproof." He grabbed the backpack and slipped it over his shoulders. "That protection from the pendant?"

"Yes. Too bad you can't get it off. You stand no chance."

James lifted his hand and concentrated. The amulet enhanced his barely-there telekinesis. He avoided the power because it didn't seem all that useful in most fire-fights, but maybe it'd help.

The pendant didn't budge. Of course.

Schwartz frowned. "What are you trying, Brownstone? Some little trick? You don't understand how many artifacts I have on me right now, and how many I've activated. The potions I've drunk. Whatever pathetic magic you've begged from Smite-Williams won't help you here. You're at my mercy. I am your god."

James dropped his hand and shrugged. "It was worth a shot." He whipped out a throwing knife and sent it straight toward the man's head, but it bounced off like the bullets before.

"I've got to say, you're a bit of a disappointment." Schwartz shrugged.

He lifted his white glove and snapped his fingers, and a purple sphere of energy winked into existence and flew toward James. The ball slammed into him, knocking him halfway across the room. The sizzle of his flesh filled his nose.

He hissed as he landed on the burned flesh of his chest. His harness fell off, and he grabbed the healing potion out of the pouch and stuck in his pocket.

"Nothing," Schwartz ranted. "Weak. Pathetic."

"Do you ever shut the fuck up?" James stood and shook his head. "Guess I'm gonna have to do this the old-fashioned way."

"Now you die." Schwartz snapped his fingers again.

Another blast tore into James. He grunted at the impact, but this time it only stung.

The amulet's excited whispers increased.

The smile fell from Schwartz's face. "What? How are you still standing?"

James grinned despite the pain in his chest. "Got to say, Schwartz, you're a bit of a disappointment. That was your big surprise? You should have killed me when you had the chance. Everyone gets one chance to kill me, but after that I make no promises. Now it's my turn."

The bounty hunter charged Schwartz. The other man flicked the wrist of the hand wearing the black glove. A blue energy blade popped into existence and sliced James' arm. He growled as his blood sprayed across the floor.

"Fuck."

Schwartz sliced at James with another blue energy blade. Pain jolted through the bounty hunter's body, but there was no new wound. "You won't win, Brownstone. You can't win against me. I'm better than you. Smarter. I see reality. You see only false hope."

"I've had enough of your shit." James rose with an uppercut. His fist slammed into Schwartz, and the white-suited man flew backward with a yelp. He crashed to the ground, rolling several times before stopping. "You're a pretty pathetic god, Schwartz."

Schwartz wiped blood off his mouth and stood. "If I hadn't been wearing the pendant that would have killed me." He glared at James. "A lucky hit, but you haven't won."

"That was the point, asshole. You wanted to convince me that you were a tough guy." James gritted his teeth at the spreading ache in his arm. "You win. I'm convinced. So now I'm gonna beat you down like I do tough guys. Your survival isn't guaranteed, though. Sorry about that, asshole."

"You're just a bounty hunter. You can't beat me."

James ignored the pain and rushed Schwartz again. His fists flew. Left. Right. Right. Left. The other man jerked under the powerful blows. The bounty hunter finished with an elbow to the man's face.

Schwartz flew backward, crashing into and embedding in the living room wall with a groan. His face was battered, and his nose askew.

The amulet murmured something in James' mind. Mockery, James thought.

*Not impressed with the competition?*

James shook out his fists. "Thought you were gonna tear me apart atom by atom, asshole. Where's all that tough shit now? I was expecting the world's greatest badass, but instead, I got some survivalist asshole with delusions of grandeur."

The other man fell to his knees, blood pouring from his mouth and nose. He spat out blood and teeth. "I'll fucking kill you, Brownstone. I will make your death slow and painful."

"You know how many times I've heard that? All you've managed is to kill my clothes, fucker." James grinned. A little cockiness was almost as good as a painkiller. "I'm pissed about the boots, though."

Schwartz reached into his pocket and pulled out a small ring. "You haven't won, Brownstone." He slipped on the ring and stood, his eyes wide and a crooked smile on his face. He ran toward the hallway.

"You're fucking trying to escape *now*?" James shook his head and jogged after him.

The hallway led to the master bedroom. Small gold,

silver, and bone figurines of animals covered a king-sized bed.

Schwartz ran to the corner of the room and turned around.

James stopped in the doorway. Maybe there were more traps.

"Got nowhere to run now, asshole."

"You're not going to win, Brownstone. Even if I die, I'll be famous as long as I take you with me."

"Is that what you want? To be famous? I thought you wanted to survive."

Schwartz tilted his head, his eyes unfocused. "Killing you will make the world a better place. You're too dangerous to live."

James snorted. "You know what? Fuck this. Why am I even bothering?"

"Fuck this?"

"Yeah. Fuck this." James patted the backpack. "I've got what I came here for, and I've busted you up. Stay the fuck away from the Professor unless you want me to finish you off, asshole." He turned on his heel and headed down the hallway.

"Don't turn your back on me when I'm talking to you, Brownstone," Schwartz shrieked.

James held up his middle finger as a response. "Fuck you."

"Die," Schwartz shrieked.

A gold, silver, and bone figurine blinked into existence a few feet in front of James.

"What the fuck?"

The gold one exploded first, knocking James back. The

silver figurine then blasted out a sphere of blue-white energy. The bone figurine vanished and released a wave of orange energy that hit the bounty hunter before he'd even landed.

Agony shot through James, and more explosions shook the house. The amulet shouted in his mind, a mixture of excitement and fear. It was enjoying him being blown up three different ways.

Wood, metal, and plastic fragments coated James. Another series of explosions launched him into the air. The pain clouded his mind, making it hard to concentrate on anything else.

The amulet grew silent, intrigued but frightened. Learning. That's what it was doing. Learning quickly about so many new forms of magic.

A massive blast wave slammed into the bounty hunter. He tumbled through the air, his skin sizzling and every nerve on fire. James slammed into the ground in agony. He forced his trembling hand into his pocket and grabbed his last healing potion.

Darkness ate at the edge of his vision, but he unstopped the bottle and downed the liquid.

The darkness overtook him and he slumped to the ground, unconscious.

"Been a nice few days," Trey announced from the middle of the living room. The rest of the boys were sitting on couches or chairs in the loft's living room. "We've had some good catches. Made some nice money. I wasn't sure about this new flexible schedule compared to what we were using before, but y'all have made me a believer, and I'm sure the big man will be."

Shorty laughed. "I don't give a shit about kicking ass either here or LA. I just like kicking ass and making money."

"We *are* badass," Deshawn declared.

"We are Brownstone badass," Travis added.

Manuel and the others nodded their agreement.

Trey grinned. "Damned right. We've got one more job tonight, then we'll head back. Should be easy." He stared at Shorty. "It's gonna be a chick. We shouldn't have to get rough, though. She's level two. She's a con artist. Only thinks she's so high because she conned some rich assholes. You gonna be okay with that?"

Shorty shrugged. "I'm fine, Trey. I shot at that witch earlier. Let's just bag this bitch, get our money, and head back."

Trey nodded. "You done good, boys. You done good."

Upping their game to multiple twos and threes in rapid succession had helped the money flow in, and the fact the Las Vegas Metropolitan Police Department was shoving bounties at them only helped. Even with splitting the bounty, giving James his cut, and paying for expenses, the Las Vegas trip had been damned profitable. Way more profitable than their best days on the street as gang members.

*This shit's nice. Really nice.*

Trey shook his head and headed toward the kitchen. He had time to grab a little snack before they went after their last bounty. It wouldn't be their first woman, and the last few had surrendered without much of a fight.

*Would Victoria surrender without a fight if we had a bounty on her?*

Trey stopped and frowned.

*I'm fucking chewing Shorty out for getting distracted by some hot ass, but now I'm thinking about some witch who was* this close *to blowing me across an alley?*

Trey snorted. It used to be he worried about Demon Generals killing his boys or attacking his family. Now he was worried about beautiful witches who hadn't even tried to kill him.

*Yeah, this ain't a bad life. Talk about your first-world problems.*

He continued toward the kitchen. Maybe he'd get lucky and run into Victoria again.

Darkness surrounded James. Without either the Devil or Jesus in sight, he was probably not dead yet. At least he hoped not.

*I'm just dreaming. Have to be.*

A woman's voice intruded in his thoughts.

"You're a dumbass, Brownstone. A tough dumbass, but still a dumbass. You have the Devil's own luck."

*Yeah. Probably.*

It wasn't Shay's voice. It was Lieutenant Hall's.

*What the fuck? Why am I dreaming about another woman? If Shay finds out, she'll gut me.*

"Wake the fuck up, Brownstone," Lieutenant Hall demanded. "You're breathing and you don't seem to be hurt, even if your clothes are torn up. Magical shit, I'm assuming."

James' eyes snapped open to find an armored but helmet-free Lieutenant Hall staring down at him, a huge frown on her face.

"Do I need to find your girlfriend, Brownstone?"

He shook his head and sat up. "No. I don't need my ass kicked again." Despite his shredded and burned clothes, he was in no pain. The potion had done its job. There was enough of his shirt left to conceal his amulet, and the blood, dust, and general grime of the battle helped hide the lines radiating from the amulet to the rest of his chest.

*Should have brought an energy potion. Fucking exhausted.*

James stood and took in his surroundings. AET and regular officers covered the area, most surrounding the charred crater where Schwartz's house had been. Men in radiation suits stood in the crater, waving Geiger counters and other instruments around.

Lieutenant Hall pointed toward the crater. "That's new. Start talking. The only reason I'm not completely pissed off is that you didn't do this shit anywhere near town."

James reached to his back. The backpack was still there. He unzipped and pulled out the golden plaque. He let out a sigh of relief.

"I don't have any fucking idea what that is," Lieutenant Hall snapped. "Or what it has to do with the large *crater* over there."

"Something for a friend." James put the plaque back into the backpack. "I was asked to pick it up. An asshole had taken it from him, and I thought it'd be a simple show-up-and-growl-type job. Things got…complicated."

"Complicated?"

James shrugged. "This asshole was a paranoid, crazy motherfucker who decided he'd rather blow me the fuck up, even after I got what I wanted and said I was leaving. He had a buttload of artifacts, too."

Lieutenant Hall let out a long sigh. "I want to believe you, Brownstone. I really do. But I'm not sure how. Right now all I have is you, a crater, and a lot of unusual magical activity. Considering how much blood you're covered with without any wounds, you were either using healing magic, or you cut someone up, and they never had a chance. I don't know if I can just let you walk."

James frowned. "My phone. Give me my phone, and I can prove it."

"Weber," Lieutenant Hall shouted. "You got Brownstone's phone from his truck, right?"

"Yeah," the sergeant called from a few yards away. He was holding a plastic bag with James' phone. He hurried over to hand the bag to James.

"You broke into my truck?" James asked, trying to keep the growl out of his voice.

*Even the cops can't fucking touch my truck.*

"Don't worry, we didn't break anything." Lieutenant Hall shrugged. "We thought you were dead until Weber saw you were breathing. We were collecting evidence. So you have your phone. What's that have to do with proof?"

"One sec." James dialed Heather.

"I thought you were dead there until you woke up just now," the hacker answered.

"You're watching me?"

"Got a couple of drones high up."

"Got any internal camera shit from the house? Video that I can show the cops?"

"I do. After the jammer was destroyed I started trying to access the house via the hardlines, and I found out I could access the electrical control itself. Turned everything back on and started watching. You're one tough of sonofabitch, Brownstone."

James grunted. "I need the video."

"Sending it now."

He held up the phone, which displayed a feed from an internal house camera, complete with audio of Schwartz's final rants. He'd grabbed and twisted the ring to initiate his final self-destruction plan.

Lieutenant Hall blew out a breath. "Okay, that should be enough, but you still need to come downtown to fill out some reports and statements. Otherwise, you're not walking."

James grunted. "Can I at least change? I've got some other clothes in my truck."

"Fine by me. Just follow me to the station after you get changed."

---

James sat in a too-small chair in the office waiting for Lieutenant Hall to return. They'd taken his statement and hadn't tried to seize the plaque.

The Professor had been more than willing to provide a statement indicating that he had hired James to recover the artifact and was ready to provide any necessary provenance documents. The bounty hunter had no idea if they were fake, but it had been enough, combined with the video and his statement, to induce the cops to not care.

The door swung open, and an unarmored Lieutenant Hall headed over to her desk and sat. "You're a lucky sonofabitch."

"What now?"

"Gregory Schwartz, your ranting thief nutjob? Turns out a level-four bounty was issued on him just a few hours ago."

"By who?"

"The Paris Police Prefecture. I'm working something so you can get credit for the bounty. Fortunately for you, it was dead-or-alive." Maria tapped the keyboard, and a mugshot of Schwartz appeared. "They say that guy was level four, but given the crater I saw, he should have been a level six. Even *you* are lucky to be alive, Brownstone."

"I didn't want a fight. That asshole did. I just wanted something he stole."

Lieutenant Hall chuckled and finished typing. "Yeah, I feel you, Brownstone. I can't remember the last time someone surrendered to AET. Maybe we should start a pool." She nodded toward the door. "You're free to go."

James nodded. "Thanks, Lieutenant."

She returned to her typing with a nod. "Sure thing, Brownstone. Try not to get blown up next time."

He grunted. "Okay."

James opened her door and headed down the hallway. Sergeant Mack waited against a wall, his arms crossed.

"Everything okay, Brownstone?" the cop asked.

"Yeah. I'm free and clear, and I'm even getting a bounty payment out of it."

Mack whistled. "Nice. We can buy an extra-nice pit now."

"Almost getting blown up has to be useful for something."

Shorty and Manuel sat in the Expedition watching people come and go from the front of the bar. Their target, Jenna Holmes, had been spotted in the place just a half-hour ago according to Trey's internet informants. The rest of the team had already spread out to cover the exits.

"I hope this shit's gonna be easy." Shorty leaned his head against the back of the driver's seat. "Haven't heard shit about her having muscle. I'm guessing she'll surrender without too much shit."

He hoped she would, anyway. It'd already been a long day, and he wasn't all that interested in chasing someone through Vegas's back alleys.

*Don't be a bitch, Jenna. Be cool. I'm hungry.*

Manuel stared out the window. "You know what our problem is?"

Shorty glanced his way. "What?"

"We're too damned good. It almost makes it boring."

Both men chuckled.

"Don't know." Shorty frowned. "You never know what's

gonna happen, you know what I'm saying? Might be an easy catch. I *think* she'll be an easy catch, but she also might be a witch or have a guy we don't know about."

"A witch? If she was a witch she'd be at least a four." Manuel shrugged. "Just because one witch slipped into a bounty don't mean every low-level bounty is gonna have some magical surprise."

"Just saying, we ain't getting paid because this shit is safe."

"Since when we ever live a safe life? When we was running on the streets, we had to deal with both the po-po and other gangs."

Shorty grinned. "Now we're in the toughest fucking gang of all."

Manuel opened his mouth to reply, but shut it and nodded toward the passenger-side window. "I think that's her."

A woman in a low-cut red dress strode out of the bar in matching knee-high boots, a huge orange purse over her shoulder.

Shorty whistled. "She don't like to blend in. Shit. Why do the hot ones always got to be trouble?"

Manuel laughed. "More fun that way, brother. Ready?"

"Yeah, ready. Let's do this shit before my stomach gnaws its way out of my body."

The bounty hunters threw open the SUV doors, stepped out, and advanced on the bounty. The heels of her boots clacked against the stairs leading to the bar as she made her way to the street.

Jenna stopped and gave them both a coy smile after

looking them up and down. "Do you gentlemen need something? I'm pretty sure I haven't seen you around before, and I think I'd remember two handsome men in suits like you."

Shorty grinned. "Yeah, sweet thing. We need something. You."

"Ooh, aren't you the direct one?" The woman eyed them. "You're not normally my type, but I can be persuaded. Tonight's been *so* boring. What do you do for a living? Businessmen?"

Shorty resisted a laugh. It was the first time in his entire life anyone had ever mistaken him for a businessman, or even anything remotely respectable.

*Shit, Trey. You win. The suits do make us look good.*

Manuel and Shorty exchanged glances, and the latter spoke. "We're bounty hunters with the Brownstone Agency. Jenna Holmes, we're taking you to the police. We don't want trouble, so if you could come along nice and quiet-like it'd save us all a headache and some scratches, you know what I'm saying?"

Shorty expected her to run or pull a gun from her purse, maybe even try to claw his eyes out. What he *didn't* expect was for her to fall to her knees and sob, her face in her hands.

*Shit. I hate crying chicks.*

He blinked a few times and looked at Manuel. The other man shrugged, confusion on his face.

Jenna continued sobbing for several minutes before regaining control and wiping her tears away. "Please, you can't do this. It's not even my fault. My asshole ex-boyfriend framed me. You're here about the level-two bounty, right? The one connected to where I was allegedly transporting a bunch of dust?"

"I don't know shit about what you did. All I was told was that you are a level two."

She shook her head. "Well, it doesn't matter. It's all crap. You should go after Zander Wainright, my ex. I'm sure if you look him up, he'll have a bounty. I didn't have anything to do with his crimes. This is bullshit, and it's unfair."

"That might be true, but if we take you to the police, they can figure it out." Shorty shrugged. "Not our job to convict you. Just our job to bring you in, sweet thing."

Manuel nodded his agreement.

Jenna stood, her knees wobbly. "Yeah, they'll figure it out while I'm stuck in jail waiting for some cartel assholes who think I stole millions of dollars of dust." She clasped her hands together and pled with her watery eyes. "Please! If I get arrested I'm dead, and it's not fair. Look Zander Wainright up. He's got a bounty. He's an actual scumbag. I broke up with him right away once I realized what he was into."

Shorty rubbed the back of his head. "I don't know."

Manuel pulled out his phone and brought up the bounty-hunting app. He tapped away.

"There's a Zander Wainright in here. He's got a level two on him. Multiple assaults, attempted murder. Drug trafficking. Fucker's nasty. Real thug."

Jenna nodded quickly. "See? Come on, I'm begging you here, guys. It's not like bringing in some level-two bounty is going to set you up for life, and if you need the money, Zander's a better choice. He's a real criminal. My only crime was dating a scumbag."

Shorty sighed and looked at Manuel.

The other bounty hunter shrugged. "We can just say we didn't see her. Not like some internet informant's always gonna be right."

Jenna's eyes widened, and she placed her palms together. "Thank you, thank you, thank you." She blew out a breath. "This has been very stressful. I think I need another drink." The woman spun on her heel and all but sprinted into the bar.

"Wait," Shorty shouted, his arm outstretched, but Jenna ignored him. "Shit. Guess she's right. One level two ain't gonna make a big difference anyway." He nodded back toward the Expedition. "Might as well wait in there."

The two men made it back to the car and sat in silence, both staring out the window. They were unsure of if Trey would believe them.

Shorty gritted his teeth a few minutes later when their leader turned the corner, pushing a handcuffed Jenna Holmes.

"Fuck my life," he muttered.

Manuel slapped a hand to his forehead and groaned.

The bounty hunters hopped out of the SUV and hurried over to the pair.

"I—" Shorty began.

Trey held up a hand. "Don't say shit. You got conned, Shorty. I know, because this bitch just tried to con me, and I know there's no way she'd be sneaking out the back unless she went out front and ran into you."

Shorty shrugged and averted his gaze.

Trey chuckled and shook his head. "My bad, Shorty. I should have briefed you better. She ain't got a level two for losing any dust. She got a level two for all her con-woman shit." He shoved her toward the Expedition. "Nice try, but no one can con a Garfield without some magic, bitch."

Jenna rolled her eyes. "I was *this close* to getting away." She batted her eyelashes. "I can still make it worth your while if you let me go."

"Please." Trey snorted. "The money they're gonna pay out for your bounty will make it worthwhile." He pushed her forward and glared at Shorty and Manuel.

Both men got into the back of the car, avoiding looking at Trey or the bounty.

Shorty sighed.

*Fuck. Can't believe I got played like that.*

---

Tyler leaned back in his chair and put his feet on his desk. Several rings sounded before the call connected.

"Who the fuck is this?" rumbled a voice over the line.

"Tyler, owner of the Black Sun. You heard of me?"

"Yeah. I know who you are. Why the fuck are you calling me?"

Tyler grinned. Time to make some money.

He cleared his throat. "I've heard some shit that I'd thought I pass along to all the level fours and higher. People who are ass-kickers like yourself, Patrick."

"I'm listening."

Tyler dropped his feet and sat up. "James Brownstone's throwing down the gauntlet. Told me he's willing to take people on. It'll be one-on-one. No AET. No other bullshit.

They beat his ass or kill him. They don't have to look over their shoulder."

Patrick snorted. "Fuck that noise. You expect me to seriously agree to walk up to Brownstone?"

"You scared, Patrick?"

"Fuck it. I've got a great rep without taking on Brownstone. If I try and go after him, there's no fucking upside for me."

Tyler smiled. "First of all, there'd be some extra money in it for you, courtesy of me. Also, you wouldn't have to worry about when he's coming because—"

Patrick hung up.

The informer broker frowned. There weren't a large number of level fours and fives in the area. Brownstone's presence in LA had seemed to scare them away in recent months, but Tyler didn't want his career as a fight promoter to be over as soon as it started. He had to try harder.

*Okay, whatever. Patrick's just one guy. I'll call the next guy. Not everyone is a pussy afraid of Brownstone.*

Tyler stared at his phone for a moment before nodding. The plan wasn't dead.

***

Two hours later, Tyler had contacted five more candidates with no more success than the first. Three men were briefly willing to consider the idea before deciding, much like Patrick, that it wasn't worth the risk to their reputations or freedom. Two others talked a lot of trash but still said no in the end.

Tyler slumped over his desk, resting his head in the palm of his free hand as he made his pitch to candidate number six.

"There'd be money for you showing up, and you'd know exactly when Brownstone would be coming and where. With that kind of information, a witch like you could take him down easily. I mean, shit…you've got a level-five bounty. And like I said, there will be no AET. This is fucking silver-platter material here."

"Are you fucking out of your mind?" the witch yelled. "You think I'm an idiot? Brownstone wouldn't even care that I'm a woman. I heard what he did to the Collector in Japan. Don't call me again." She hung up.

Tyler scrubbed a hand over his face. Why weren't people greedier? Half these people could destroy a city block by themselves, but were wetting their pants because he suggested they take on James Brownstone in a deserted area.

*Sure, the guy kicks a lot of ass, but he's just a man in the end. He's not a freaking god. Maybe I need to spin that he won't kill them if he can avoid it.*

The info broker dropped his head to his desk. Guaranteeing they wouldn't die would only scare people off. Where was an arrogant fuck like King Pyro when he needed him?

---

Thirty minutes later Tyler pulled his phone back to stare at it, convinced he hadn't heard right.

He put the phone back to his ear. "What did you just say?"

"I'll do it," rumbled Lars on the other end. "But I get to pick the place, date, and time. That way I know there'll be no Brownstone bullshit tricks."

Tyler thrust his fist into the air in triumph. Lars might have been his last hope, but the man was a level five. The info broker could make a lot of money off this fight if he set things up right.

"Brownstone wants to pick the place. I know where he's going do it. It's fucking far away from anywhere in LA. He wants to make sure no random people are hurt, and I can guarantee there will be no AET."

Lars grunted. "Fine. Don't give a fuck, then. If we fight in the city, those AET assholes will show to spoil all the fun. Make sure you pass that along to that fucker Brownstone, and we'll talk soon about when I'm gonna end his ass. You better not be shitting about the money. You fuck with me, I don't give a shit about your place's neutrality. I'll walk into that bar and flatten it, AET guarantees or not."

*Don't fucking threaten me, asshole. I hope Brownstone knocks you around a lot.*

Tyler shook his head instinctively, despite being on the phone. "Nope. You'll get a flat fee plus a percentage of the gross receipts from the bets. Not only that, you'll go down as the man who took down James Brownstone."

"Damn right. Now I got shit to do." Lars ended the call.

Tyler set his phone down and rubbed his hands together. No matter how this ended, he would make sure he made money.

*I'm so damned brilliant.*

14

Carl yawned from the middle seat of the Expedition. "I thought you said Holmes was the last one tonight. We're kicking ass, Trey. Not like we need to kick *all* the ass, though."

Trey forced himself not to yawn, even if fatigue tugged at his eyes and muscles.

He shook his head as he pulled the SUV in front of a modest home. "I thought about that, but then I got a tip that this asshole was staying here. Only a level one, so I figured, why not just drop by and pick up some free cash? Ignoring it would be like ignoring a Hamilton on the sidewalk."

Several of the other bounty hunters grumbled but stopped once Trey shot them a glare. This had always been a problem with his boys in their gang days. They were brave and tough but could be lazy if he let them.

"Don't be pussies. It's like the staff sergeant told you. When it's time to play you do what you need to do, but when it's time to work you deliver the goods, even if you're tired as fuck."

Carl shrugged. "We ain't Marines, Trey."

"Nah, we're just bounty hunters working for James Brownstone, so we should be trying to be *more* badass than Marines." Trey threw open the door. "Now surround the fucking house, so the bounty don't get away. Or you can stay here and suck your thumbs."

The front door of the home opened before all the men exited the vehicle. Trey grabbed for his gun, but the emergence of an old woman in a robe, her hair up in curlers, had him dropping his hand a second later.

*Hope that nana ain't no witch.*

"You Mafia?" the woman called. She frowned and looked at each of the men. "Or work for them?"

Trey straightened his tie and gave her a winning smile. Time for Smooth Trey. "No, ma'am. We don't associate with such disreputable people. We're firmly on the side of the law, you see."

The woman frowned, her eyes darting back and forth. "Then why you here? Don't try to feed me a line and tell me you're here to sell me religion. I don't need religion, and I know thugs when I see them."

Several of the men frowned. Manuel winced.

*Thugs? Bitch, please. I'm trying to be nice here.*

Trey kept smiling. "We're not thugs, ma'am. We're with the Brownstone Agency. We just want to talk with William, and we've been informed he's staying here." He shrugged. "He's got a bounty on him, ma'am. If he comes with us nice and quiet-like, we guarantee we won't harm a hair on his head. But you should know that the word's out that he's in town, and some much less nice men might show up. It's a win-win for him to come with us."

The old woman snorted. "The word's old." She nodded toward the house. "Go ahead and check if you want. He ain't here anymore."

Trey chuckled. "You expect me to believe that?"

She gestured toward her open front door. "Like I said, go ahead and check. Not saying he was never here. He was staying with me, but then he heard that Brownstone's thugs were in town so he ran. Little chickenshit. I raised him to be tougher than that. I almost hope you catch his ass now and beat him down. It'd serve him right for being a pussy."

"Seriously?" Trey glanced at the other bounty hunters. They all shrugged.

He locked eyes with the defiant old woman. Her story rang true. She wasn't sweating, fidgeting, or averting her gaze.

"Damn it," Trey muttered. "You got any idea where your boy ran off to?"

"Nope." The woman shook her head. "If I knew, I'd tell you. Now, you gonna ransack my house, or are you gonna leave me alone? Don't have time for this thug crap. I was in the middle of watching *CSI: Oriceran.*"

Trey gave her a polite nod. "Nah, we got no reason to mess with you over a level one. Enjoy your show." He gestured toward the car. "Come on, boys. It's a bust."

The others fell in behind him, a few muttering under their breaths. Soon they were back on the road.

Shorty sighed from the back seat. "That was bullshit. Total fucking bullshit."

Trey glanced up at his rearview mirror. Shorty's face was pressed into a tight frown.

"You think we should have busted up her house?" Trey asked. "The big man wouldn't like us doing that kind of shit, especially over a level one."

Shorty shook his head. "That ain't what I'm saying. She called us thugs. We got suits and licenses. We've been trained by a Marine. We ain't thugs."

Every man in the SUV wore a mask of annoyance or concern.

Carl ran his hand along his tie. "Hell, we *were* thugs, but we ain't thugs now. We're on the side of the law, so how can that bitch say that? This is some messed-up shit."

"Bounties' families ain't gonna like us," Trey announced as he pulled to a stop at a red light. "But it didn't bother y'all before when we actually *were* thugs. So why the fuck do you care now what some old woman who ain't your nana says?"

"Before we were thugs." Shorty shrugged. "Now we ain't. It's supposed to be different. People supposed to treat us different. With respect, you know what I'm saying?"

Manuel let out a long sigh. "I think I need to drown my ego in about a gallon of God Sauce."

The light turned green and Trey accelerated. "Maybe they'll give us a thug discount on top of our Brownstone discount."

---

Tyler paced back and forth in his office, every muscle tense with excitement. His fight-promotion career was actually taking off.

*I can make piles of money off this if I work this right—and if Brownstone can manage not to die. It's like I can't lose lately.*

He dialed Brownstone.

"Yeah?" the bounty hunter rumbled by way of answering.

Tyler stopped pacing. "I've got a guy. A level five. Lars Hansen. He's willing to do it, but he gets to call the date and time."

The silence stretched on, and Tyler's jaw tightened and he started pacing again.

"Okay," Brownstone finally answered. "But I still want to do the Salton Sea. Not going somewhere if the fucker gets to pick the place."

"That's fine." Tyler laughed. "You sure about this, Brownstone? This guy's a level five. This isn't going to be one of your show-up-and-throw-a-punch deals. The guy is probably as strong as you, and can basically turn his skin to stone."

Brownstone grunted. "I'd end up going after him anyway. This just saves me the trouble of tracking his ass down.

"Glad you see it that way."

"I assume you're gonna be setting up bets?"

"You're damned right I'm going to be setting up bets. There's no way I'm going to pass up the opportunity to make money." Tyler blinked, and he frowned. "Fuck."

"What?"

Tyler groaned. "I have to bet on you, don't I?" He sighed and dropped into his chair.

Brownstone chuckled. "You don't *have* to."

"I'll fucking lose money if I don't. Whatever. If you want to bet, though, you need to come down to the Black Sun to place them in person."

"Why?"

"Because I want that money in case you get killed, and it'll help people see I'm in control." Tyler grinned, his earlier concern over having to bet on his nemesis swallowed by the joy of control.

"Fine," Brownstone answered. "I'll be there soon."

---

A murmur swept over the Black Sun as Tyler filled in the boxes he'd set up on the old dusty chalkboard that served him so well during the last few betting pools. It was time to define the possible bets and get the money flowing in.

"What's going on?" a man called from the bar. "You gonna be taking bets again? On Brownstone, or something else?"

Tyler looked over his shoulder. "You're damned right I'm gonna be taking bets. And, yeah, James Brownstone's gonna be taking on Lars Hansen. This is going to be a match for the ages."

"Shit. The level five? Last I heard, he was in Wyoming."

"Nope." Tyler scribbled BROWNSTONE VS. HANSEN across the top of the chalkboard. "He's in LA, and Brownstone and him are going to fight. Hansen's a nasty customer. Probably as strong as Brownstone, and just as tough. He demolished an Atlanta AET team a couple of years back all by himself, you know."

A huge biker at a table set his beer down. "Shit. That was him?"

Tyler grinned. "Yep. Lars has made it clear he's not afraid of Brownstone, and given his history, this is the first time in a long time that I think we've got a serious chance of the Granite Ghost being taken down."

*Fuck. If Brownstone was gone I'd be a lot happier, but without him, I'll be losing out on a lot of opportunities to make cash. Why does it have to be this way?*

The bar owner continued scribbling on the odds board. Different results, different odds. Surrender. Death. Maiming. Various categories for battle lengths. This elaboration continued for a couple of minutes until he realized silence had swept the room.

"Someone's here to see you, Tyler," Kathy called from the bar.

The info broker swallowed and slowly turned around. Brownstone stood behind him.

The bartender nodded to the bounty hunter, his tension melting. "Hey, Brownstone."

Everyone started murmuring and whispering at their tables. More than a few looked shocked at the casual exchange.

Brownstone stared at the chalkboard. "This your latest odds board?"

"Yeah."

The bounty hunter reached into his jacket and Tyler's stomach tightened. Maybe he'd been wrong. Maybe the bounty hunter'd had enough of the info broker's shit and changed this mind.

Brownstone pulled out a wad of cash and tossed it to

Tyler.

"What the fuck?" shouted the biker. He jumped to his feet. "Brownstone's in on it?"

He sat once the bounty hunter glared at him.

"I'm not betting on any shit other than I win."

Tyler pocketed the cash. "Fair enough, but I have to let you know you're missing a lot of nice hedge and bonus opportunities." He tapped a few of the length and injury categories with a piece of chalk.

Brownstone snorted. "Don't give a shit. This asshole's going down. I already checked his bounty. He's a dead-or-alive, so I'm not gonna hold back."

"Not my problem if you do." Tyler shrugged. "Just make sure you're at the right place at the right time."

The bounty hunter turned and stomped toward the door.

The biker glanced at Tyler and Brownstone. "I can't fucking believe this. I expected them to yell at each other, or at least some ass-kicking, but they're working together now."

Tyler gave him a smug smile. "The Black Sun isn't what it once was. *I'm* not what I once was."

*Nah, Brownstone. You can't die yet. You need to live until I've made every last penny I possibly can off you."*

---

James turned the corner in his F-350. He needed some barbeque to wash the stink of the Black Sun off him.

*What the fuck am I doing partnering with Tyler?*

The bounty hunter shook his head. Tyler's original

pitch had made sense. Taking down a level five well away from the city would earn James a pile of money, and help him remove a dangerous man from circulation. Letting the information broker facilitate matters didn't change the overall situation.

James' hand drifted to the amulet. It currently was separated from his chest with a metal spacer. Hours and hours of wearing the thing had worn him down, and it was getting harder to ignore the whispers, especially the more he thought he understood.

*I don't think Alison meant I should stay bonded with the thing all the time. At least I don't think so. Until she shows up I'll mix it up, and she can chew me out when she gets here.*

His phone rang with a call from Shay, and he winced before answering in it on speakerphone.

*Shit. If I tell her what's going on she'll freak out.*

"Hey," James rumbled.

Shay yawned on the other end. "You know what I realized today?"

"What?" He did a quick check of his mirrors for tails. Showing up at the Black Sun and placing a bet might have given some idiots ideas about taking him on. He didn't spot anyone, though.

"I learned why I'm a tomb raider and not an archaeologist. I don't mean a field archaeologist, I mean the real-deal kind I tell all my friends I am."

James changed lanes. He had only a few more blocks until the barbeque place. "What do you mean?"

"Real archaeology is a lot of research, which I do already, but it's also a lot of digging in the dirt. More shovels than magic, and that shit is tiring."

He chuckled. "Your current job not exciting enough?"

"Something like that." Shay sighed. "But enough about me. I want to talk about you."

"What about me?"

Movement caught James attention, but it was just a man in a Statue of Liberty costume spinning a large arrow sign declaring a liquidation sale at a furniture store.

"You having any trouble with the Harriken?" Shay inquired.

James grunted. "No Harriken left."

"Gangs? Mafia? Drow? Experimental dark mutants?"

He was closer now. He could practically smell the barbeque. "Nope, nope, nope, and nope."

*Yeah, Lars Hansen isn't any of those things, so it's not like I'm lying.*

Shay let out a sigh of relief. "Glad to hear you're not gonna try to get yourself killed when I'm gone. I can't always trust you to not do that."

James slowed to turn into the parking lot of the barbeque place, Jose's Grill. "I never 'try to get myself killed,' and I haven't been killed yet. Hell, I've died fewer times than you."

The tomb raider snorted. "Very funny. Okay, sounds good. If anything happens, let me know."

"Will do."

"I love you, you know."

James grunted. "Same here." He parked the F-350 and killed the engine.

He scrubbed a hand over his face. *Shay can never know about this Bounty Hunter Beat-Down Challenge.*

15

James eyed the tied-up plastic bag containing his extra order of ribs as he started the F-350 and prepared to pull out of the parking lot. Jose's ribs had satisfied him enough that he wanted to relive the meal the next morning, or maybe even later that night.

*For all I know, I might have to go kick that bounty's ass tonight. Nice to have a little pre-game meal.*

His phone rang, and he frowned when the caller ID showed Zoe's name.

James picked up the phone. "Hey, Zoe."

"It's my favorite flame," the witch purred. She giggled. "Sorry. I was doing some rather potent magic earlier. I'm a bit drunk even by my standards."

James lowered the phone and turned on speakerphone. He could drive and talk well enough at the same time.

"What's going on, Zoe?"

"Recipe tweaking."

James backed his truck out of the parking space and turned to exit the lot. "What do you mean?"

"For your potions, silly. You see, the problem is that there's something special about you. That's always made preparing potions for you more complicated than normal."

*You don't know the half of it.*

James turned onto the street. "Yeah, so? You've told me that before. I've never had any problems with your potions. Why did you need to tweak them?"

"Oh, I get that, but I've been thinking I can make them even better, and now I have. You could probably lose an arm and reconnect it with the help of one of them now. I'm rather good at what I do, if I do say so myself."

James snorted and joined the flow of street traffic. "Let's just say I'm not gonna try that shit anytime soon, and I'm still not sure if you tweaking the formula is a good thing or a bad thing."

*Shit. I wonder if tweaking the formula's gonna mess anything up with the amulet. Hell of a time to find out.*

"It's an excellent thing, I assure you." Zoe let out a merry laugh. "I'm eager for you to try them out soon. Not that I want you to hurt yourself, but I'm curious."

James grunted. "I've got…something coming up anyway. How about I stop by tomorrow morning to pick up a six-pack?"

Zoe gasped. "Six? Are you planning to destroy a city, James?"

"Nah. If everything goes right, I won't be anywhere near a city. Just got a nasty bounty to take out, and everyone keeps telling me to be careful and prepared and shit. I'm trying to take that advice to heart."

The loud sound of the witch clapping came over the line. "Okay. I've only got a few ready, so I'll have to spend some time tonight working. But I'm more than happy to do it. Talk to you later."

"Hey, you don't—"

The potions witch hung up before James could finish the sentence.

He shrugged and accelerated. As long as the bounty didn't call him out tonight, he'd be fine.

---

James scrubbed at his teeth with his toothbrush. The amulet sat on the side of his sink, still attached to the metal spacer. He stared at it, half-expecting an eye to open on it.

*Fuck. It'll be kind of creepy sleeping next to this thing. I wonder if I should give it a name other than Whispering Amulet of Doom.*

James finished brushing his teeth and rinsed. He'd made a promise to Alison, but that didn't mean he was ready to accept the amulet as part of his daily routine. He *could* keep it with him, though.

He snatched up the amulet and headed toward his bed.

*House feels empty without Shay and Alison here. Then again, don't know what Shay would say about the amulet. Probably tell me to call it Whispy Doom or something.*

He chuckled and slid the amulet underneath his pillow.

"Don't fuck up my dreams, asshole. I need to concentrate for the next few days."

As if responding to his words, his phone rang. James reached over to the nightstand, expecting Shay. The call was from a blocked number.

He glared at the pillow. "You better not be fucking

calling me to whisper at me." He tapped the phone to answer. "Who the fuck is this?"

A feminine snort sounded on the other end. "You're an asshole half the time I call, Mr. Brownstone," Heather responded. "Just thought I'd point that out."

James grunted. "Oh, well, give me a head's up that it's you rather than this blocked-number shit. It's not like you're the only one who calls me and hides their number."

"Oh, know some other hackers?"

"Yeah, but it's more like bounties and criminals who like to threaten me." James sat on the edge of the bed. "Shit gets annoying."

"Brave souls."

"Stupid fuckers, but it's all perspective." James shifted the phone. "It's kind of late. I haven't gotten any more Parkour Penny alerts, so what's this about?"

Heather sighed.

James hadn't expected any more videos of Parkour Penny given that Shay was out of town, but maybe the hacker had turned up something new she hadn't found before.

"I'm in a little bind," she explained after another sigh. "And I think I need help. Your kind of help."

"We don't know each other well enough to work on favors, so unless this involves a bounty, I don't know that I'm interested." James frowned and flipped up his pillow. The amulet still sat there. It hadn't crawled away.

Heather let out a sigh of relief. "Oh, well, that's not a problem. Because that's exactly what I have after me—a lovely bounty you could smack around and take into a local police department for a fine monetary reward."

The bounty hunter dropped the pillow. "Okay, I'm listening. What happened?"

James figured the bounty couldn't be anything high-level. Probably a one, maybe a three if he were connected to organized crime or a terrorist group.

"When I was poking into the systems of that crazy guy in San Gabriel Valley, someone else was poking around, too. I thought they were amateurs, but they were better than I expected and I tipped them off that someone else was there."

"And they're after you?" James frowned.

"They're poking around. They haven't found me yet. I did a little digging and found that the hacker's associated with a team of artifact thieves. He's a merc, but he's a good merc. I guess that explains why they were looking into Schwartz. I also know that the head guy of the group has been asking around on forums about Schwartz and hacking. I figure if the head guy goes down, the merc hacker will wander off."

James stood. He was sitting on Shay's side, and something about that made him uncomfortable. He began making his way around the bed.

"Artifact thieves?" he asked. "That means they have magic?"

"Best I can tell, they're ruthless but not that good. This artifact thief thing is a new career path for them. The main guy, Eddie Green, is a level three. He's got a couple of buddies he hangs out with who are level twos. Eddie's a piece of work, though. Nasty guy, multiple murders." Heather's voice quivered as she delivered the last sentence.

James made his way to his side of the bed and sat. "You sound pretty freaked."

Heather scoffed. "What? You expected me not to be freaked?"

"You don't seem all that easy to scare."

The hacker let out a long sigh. "Normally, I wouldn't be."

"What's different about this time?" James laid his head on his amulet-concealing pillow.

The silence dragged on for a long moment before Heather finally answered, "I'm not scared for me. I'm scared for my four-year-old son, Mr. Brownstone."

The bounty hunter bolted upright. "You have a son?"

*Shit. I thought she was just some kid playing around like Peyton.*

"Yeah, I have a son. It's not like they've tagged me directly, but they are still looking around, and just my luck, the assholes are based out of my city. I've found some stuff on the dark web that makes me think Green blames me for him losing out on an artifact haul."

James snorted. "Like the assholes were gonna get anything from Schwartz. They wouldn't have made it past his front gate."

"I know, right? But it doesn't matter. I can't take the risk of someone coming after me and my son getting caught in the crossfire. So I'm asking you, Mr. Brownstone, to do your thing. Not a favor, just come and take down some bounties. If I know you're coming, I can leak enough information to get them somewhere easy for you to pick off."

"Fine," James rumbled. "But if I'm doing this, shit has to change. I'm done with this blocked number subterfuge shit.

If I'm gonna be working with you, we need to know each other."

"Fair enough. I'm willing to meet you face-to-face wherever you want in San Francisco."

"San Francisco? Couldn't you have been a little closer?" James chuckled.

"I could have been in Sweden."

The bounty hunter snorted. "Okay, fine. You pick a place, a restaurant, and send me the address. I don't give a shit where, as long as it isn't some rabbit food crap. Go ahead and lay out the trail for Eddie and his buddies. If everything goes well after the meeting, I'll clean that shit up right away."

"I know just the place." Heather let out a sigh of relief. "I appreciate this, Mr. Brownstone."

"If we're gonna trust each other, why don't you just call me James?"

"Okay, James. I'll send you an address in a few minutes." She hung up.

James frowned down at the phone, wondering if the hacker might be setting him up. He shook his head. She'd already had plenty of chances to fuck him over, and it didn't matter anyway.

He reached under the pillow and grabbed the amulet. He'd have the bad boy with him if he needed it.

*Shit. Better let Shay know what I'm up to.*

James tapped in a quick text.

**Taking a trip tomorrow to San Francisco to capture a bounty.**

His phone chimed with an immediate reply.

**Level?**

**Just three, with two friends.**

**Oh. Be careful. Kind of busy, so can't chat right now, but if you let a level three kill you I'm gonna mock you at your funeral.**

**I'll keep that in mind.**

James tossed his phone on the nightstand and hid the amulet under his pillow again. Tomorrow was going to be a busy day.

16

Tyler polished the bar with a rag in his free hand while he kept his phone to his ear with the other. "I just wanted to confirm that you're still down for this, Lars. We can both make a lot of money, but I understand if you're afraid of Brownstone."

A little prodding always helped move things along.

Lars snorted on the other end. "Fuck Brownstone. This is gonna be the beat-down of the century, and he'll be crying like a baby before I finish his ass. How are the bets coming?"

"Word is spreading. Might want to give it another day so we can get more money sloshing around." Tyler glanced at the odds board.

"You know what? Fuck your fees."

The info broker blinked. "Huh? You want to do it for free? Not that I'm complaining, but just don't want you to leave money you have coming on the table."

"Nah. Still want it, but I'm gonna stop by and place a big bet, too. Might as well take money from all the Brownstone-betting suckers after I kill his ass." Lars grunted. "You never told me where this shit's gonna be."

"I'm going to send you some GPS coordinates for the exact place, but it's going to be in the Salton Sea area." Tyler finished his polishing and tossed his rag into a bin underneath the bar. "Not going to be a lot of rocks or places to hide out there. Is that going to be a problem? Don't know all that much about your style."

Lars snorted. "Fuck, no. I don't want that shit Brownstone trying anything. I like everything nice and open. When you're a badass, you don't need to hide." He gave a dark chuckle. "I'll give him a day more, and then I'm calling out that bitch. Send those coordinates to me now, though."

"Sure. No problem. I'll send them in a few minutes."

"See you tomorrow, Tyler." Lars hung up.

Tyler shook his head and pocketed his phone. Lars might be a level five, but the bastard was getting cocky. He needed to take his opponent more seriously. If the event was a one-sided beat-down, the info broker wouldn't be able to make a lot of money off the video.

*Wonder if there's a way I can sell merchandise? Maybe not on this fight, but for future ones. T-Shirts, maybe?*

He'd decided against relying on Brownstone to set up any of the cameras. He was going to make a not-so-quick trip to the battle area to get a few cameras and drones ready. Brownstone hadn't seemed to care when he'd texted to tell him.

Tyler stared at the odds board standing in front of the wall. He took a deep breath and rang a bell he'd purchased earlier that day and mounted above the bar.

Everyone stopped talking to look at him.

"Just got off the phone with Lars Hansen. He's eager to get going on this. We're going to have a Brownstone-and-Hansen fight, gentlemen. Still not too late to place bets."

Cheers rose.

A few cops in the corner frowned at him but didn't rise from their table.

*This is a neutral place, guys. I'm not doing anything wrong here, and Maria has bet before on this kind of thing.*

*Not even doing anything illegal. Well, not seriously illegal. Just arranging for Brownstone to do what he always does. This isn't any different than what the city did with the Harriken organizational bounty.*

Tyler smirked. He needed to start making a list of all the things he was going to do with his winnings.

---

"I always forget how fucking far away this city is," James grumbled under his breath as he took his exit off I-5. "California is too damned big."

The Secret Sauce, the barbeque place Heather had chosen, was only ten minutes from the exit. A small comfort, but after hours on the highway, James would take it.

Her last text had told him to go to the Secret Sauce and the time, and that she would meet him there. She even insisted that "He would know her when he saw her."

James snorted at the thought. It might be a dumbass move, but if shit got too hot he could duck into a closet and bond with his amulet.

The actual bounty was a nasty piece of work, but nothing

James couldn't handle. He doubted he'd even need to pull a weapon, assuming the asshole hadn't gotten his hands on any badass artifact since the last reports about him.

The truck hit a steep hill. James crested it, then drifted down. Only a few minutes to the restaurant.

A mirror check revealed nothing other than terrible drivers. Nailing him right after the exit would have been the best move if the whole thing were a setup.

The Secret Sauce was a small, modest building in a strip mall. James pulled into a convenient parking spot right in front of the restaurant. He checked his gun and ran his hand over the amulet before stepping out of his truck.

*Guess it's time to see what's up.*

His phone chimed with a text from Tyler.

**Everything's still on. Probably going to happen tomorrow. I got the recording equipment already set up like I told you I would, so you don't have to worry about that.**

James snorted.

*Asshole probably thought I couldn't handle it.*

The bounty hunter decided to test the theory that brevity was the soul of wit with his response.

**OK.**

Notes of cayenne and vinegar reached James' nose, summoning a wave of relaxation that swept through his muscles. Hard to be tense when you smelled good barbeque.

James opened the door and stepped inside. The bounty hunter surveyed the room but didn't spot a woman. He shrugged and dropped into a chair at a table.

The small dining room had only eight tables, and the only one occupied held a large man who was going to town on brisket.

A smiling waiter pushed out of the back and headed toward his table. "We don't get a lot of celebrities in here." He pulled out his phone and held it up. "Mind if I get a picture, Mr. Brownstone?"

James shrugged. He'd gotten used to this sort of thing. "Knock yourself out."

The man eating brisket glanced his way but then returned his attention to his meat.

*That's how shit should be in a barbeque place. Fuck celebrities. Barbeque's the most important thing.*

The waiter snapped a photo of James and pocketed his phone. "I'd recommend, for a man of your discerning tastes, our Trip Around the Carolinas pork platter. One-third East Carolina, one-third North, one-third South. Comes with fries."

James shook his head. "I don't care about the fries, but that sounds good."

"I'll be back soon, Mr. Brownstone."

---

Twenty minutes later, James licked the sauce off his fingers. The restaurant wasn't Jessie Rae's, but it was hitting the spot.

The brisket commando had already left but had asked for a selfie right before his departure. James obliged, but couldn't help but notice that he was now alone in the dining room. It was an excellent opportunity for an abrupt RPG, fireball, or machine gun attack.

James glowered through the window. Anyone daring to blow up a barbeque restaurant had better hope they found a portal to Oriceran as soon as possible. Only a few things in his life were sacred, but the church and barbeque were high on his list.

The bounty hunter returned to his trip through the Carolinas, only taking his attention off his delicious sauce-covered pork when the door opened.

A small boy who looked to be around four or five stepped inside and held the door open. A pretty twenty-something black-haired woman in a wheelchair rolled in next.

James stared at her, surprised. She rolled his way, the boy trailing her.

The bounty hunter set his most recent victim, an East Carolina rib, back on his tray. "Heather?"

The woman gave him a faint smile. "Not what you expected?"

The boy pulled up a chair beside his mother and sat, watching James.

James shrugged. "I don't know what I expected. Maybe someone with a lot of tattoos who wore hoodies or something?" He glanced toward the boy. "Finding out about him the other day was a surprise."

The boy reached for a rib with a question in his eyes.

James nodded. "Go ahead, kid. I've got plenty."

The boy smiled and snatched a rib from the tray. Hard to hate a kid who understood the deliciousness of barbeque.

Heather sighed. "Thanks for coming, James. I wasn't sure if you would."

"If I didn't want to come I would have said so. I don't do bullshit games." He frowned and gestured toward her legs. "But yeah, kind of surprised by that."

"You never thought a hacker might be disabled?"

James shook his head. "Just these days, even if you can't get something fixed by normal doctors, you can usually use magic. You still have your legs, so someone could do something for you."

Heather sighed. "Magic isn't that different than medicine, though. It can go wrong. Not only that, it's expensive. I can't risk spending a bunch of money on expensive magic that might not even work, especially when I need that money to take care of my son and…hide."

The waiter came by, and James ordered another tray. He waited for the man to depart before continuing.

"Why hide, though? This Eddie ass…" He glanced at the boy, but the child seemed more interested in his food than James' mouth. "You didn't have a problem with Eddie until recently."

Heather sighed. "Sure. I have a problem with him in that he's looking my way, but I've poked around in a lot of big systems, and it's not like my job is strictly legal. It's better that I keep a low profile, just in case someone's looking for me. You never know. I'm careful normally, but I let my guard down when I helped you with Schwartz. I think I let that psycho rattled me."

"Not gonna tell you how to live your life, but I can help you with Eddie at least."

The waiter returned with another large tray of

barbeque and set it down on the table, along with more napkins.

James grabbed another rib. "So, you said you could get Eddie and his guys somewhere easy for me to catch them. Did you do that?" He took a bite. Too much cayenne this time. He frowned.

Heather nodded. "Yes. They're at a bar a few miles from here. They are waiting for, well, *me* to show up, though they think I'm a guy."

"And you're sure they're still there?"

She pulled out her phone and brought up a camera feed. A scarred muscular man with a buzzcut sat at a table drinking a beer. Two rough-looking men sat with him.

James set his food down, licked his fingers, and then used a napkin to wipe them off. He stood. "Make sure no one takes my tray. I don't think this will take long." He headed out the door.

Heather wiped away a tear, all the tension in her muscles and stomach releasing. It'd been a long time since she had screwed up so badly, let alone put her son at risk. She patted her lap and smiled at her son. "Do you want to sit with Mommy and watch the bad guys get beat up?"

"Yes, Mommy." Her son hurried over to her.

*Please, James. I know you can stop these guys.*

17

James pulled into the bar's parking lot. Judging by the cars and trucks filling the area, not many people had left in the few minutes it'd taken him to drive from the Secret Sauce to the bar.

*Fuck. This isn't the Black Sun. Don't want to fuck this place up just because some assholes are in it.*

He reached toward the amulet, but then dropped his hand. It was nice to not have to deal with the whispers, and he didn't need that kind of power for a level three and a couple of levels twos.

No grenades. No knives. The only things other than his gun he needed to bring to the party were a few extra zip ties.

After nodding, the bounty hunter hopped out of his F-350 and strode into the crowded bar. A loud country song blared from the speakers, and more than a few men in flannel and cowboy boots looked his way before returning to their conversations and drinks. The crowd was nothing more than regular men and women having a good time and enjoying their drinks.

A few more people glanced his way and he saw recognition on the faces of some, but no one approached him.

Eddie and his goons radiated menace, which explained why the tables near them were empty.

James marched over to the bartender. He wanted to make the situation clear.

The bartender looked up. "What can I get for you… Oh shit." His eyes widened. He swallowed, and his gaze flicked toward Eddie's table. "You're here for them, aren't you? Look, man, I don't want any trouble here. We're not a criminal bar. They just showed up here. Never seen them before."

"Then just stay out of the way and don't piss me off."

The bartender nodded, and James stomped over to Eddie's table. He needed to clear the assholes out before he could let loose.

The bounty looked up with a smug smile. "Now, lookie here. This is some shit I did not expect. The fabulous Scourge of Harriken himself in San Fran? You get around, Brownstone. Detroit, Vegas and now San Francisco."

James grunted. "Don't be an idiot. You know how this shit goes down, Eddie."

The other man laughed and shrugged. His friends laughed, too.

Eddie grinned. "Do I, Brownstone? Do I *really*?"

"I don't want trouble. The easy thing would be for you and your buddies here to give up. I'll take you to the cops, and no one gets hurt."

Eddie ran his tongue between his teeth. "No one gets

hurt? Where's the fucking fun in that?" He traced his scar with his thumb. "Sometimes you feel the most alive when you get hurt. I think I want to feel alive, but I really want *you* to feel alive.""

"So this isn't gonna go down easy? You're gonna be a dumbass?"

"No fucking way I'll surrender to you, Brownstone."

James shrugged. "Fine. You're right. It'll be more fun that way for me." He nodded toward the door. "How about we take this outside, then?"

"Why? You afraid of all these people seeing your ass get kicked?"

"Nope." The bounty hunter pointed at the bartender. "If you win, you might want a drink after."

*Come on, asshole. Take the bait.*

Eddie chuckled and pushed himself up. "Fine, then, Brownstone, but let me be clear. I'm not saying you're not gonna die out there. I like your style, but you made the mistake of getting in my face, and I figure you're also the guy who got in the middle of my business with Schwartz."

James grunted and headed toward the door. "You should be glad I took care of Schwartz."

"Come on, boys. Let's go have a discussion with the fabulous James Brownstone."

Noah snuggled against his mother. "What's going on, Mommy? Are those men going after Mr. Brownstone?"

Heather held her phone in front of them. The audio

wasn't great, but she could follow what was being said at the table.

"Yes. Mr. Brownstone is going to take care of them. Then we won't have to worry about them."

Noah looked up at her. "Why are they bad men?"

"Because they hurt people, and they might want to hurt you or me."

Heather had tried to shield her son from this sort of thing, but it was important that he know the truth of what was going on. They'd probably never have a normal life, and the sooner he accepted that, the better.

*I know I screwed up, but James can still make this right.*

Noah looked back down at the screen and frowned. "Why don't he just beat them up right away?"

"Because he doesn't want to cause trouble for anyone else."

The waiter came up behind them. "Is there… Oh, is this live?"

Heather looked over her shoulder and nodded. "Yes."

"I've seen stuff from news helicopters with Brownstone or drone footage, but never something that close." The waiter pulled up a chair beside them. "Those guys don't look that scared, do they? Do you think they recognize him?"

"They recognize him. They just think they can beat him."

The waiter scoffed. "Idiots."

James stepped out of the bar. Eddie and his two cronies followed a few seconds later.

"Oh, darn. We don't get to see it." The waiter sighed.

Noah stuck out his lip. "I wanna see Mr. Brownstone beat up the bad men."

Heather smiled at her son. "Don't worry. I've got this." A few quick swipes and taps brought up a feed from an external camera and a low-flying drone of hers circling on a preprogrammed flight path. She needed to see it, if only to verify the end of the threat.

"Yay!" Noah clapped.

The waiter joined him.

James kept walking away from the building until he stood in the middle of the parking lot, a frown on his face. He cracked his knuckles. Eddie and his men sauntered toward him, chuckling like they were about to have a dance-off and not a fight.

Heather sighed. Eddie had no clue who he was about to fight.

James frowned. He'd convinced the bounties to leave the building, but there were still a lot of cars around. He'd need to make sure that he confined himself to the emptier area of the parking lot. If there was one thing he appreciated, it was a man's love for his car or truck.

He stepped toward the less populated part of the lot.

"Where the fuck you going, Brownstone?" Eddie called. "Running already? I haven't even done anything yet."

His cronies laughed.

The bounty hunter didn't respond until he reached his destination. "Just wanted somewhere with more room."

"More room?" Eddie started toward him. His men fell

in on either side. "Damn, Brownstone, for an alleged badass, you're sure a fussy bitch."

"My girlfriend thinks I have OCD. Maybe she's right." James shook his head. "Still doesn't have to go down like this, Eddie. You can give up right now."

He didn't care about hurting Eddie, but there was still a major risk of property damage.

The bounty laughed. "You know what, Brownstone? I think you're full of shit, and not so tough." The man punched at the air a few times. "Check it out, Brownstone. Did you know I used to box?" He nodded at his friends in turn. "These guys, well, they didn't grow up playing Parcheesi. We're tough fuckers, even without our guns."

"That mean you're not gonna try and shoot me?"

"Nah. Not yet, anyway. Where's the fun in that? You see, I've got a theory about you, Brownstone. I've read a lot about it on the internet. People agree with my idea." Eddie jabbed at the air a few more times and grinned. "You know what my theory is?"

"What? That you're a complete dumbass?"

"Nah." Eddie laughed. "My theory is you're nothing. You're shit. That you're a big lie. A trick the cops are playing on all us. They help you take down people but give you all the credit, so then you can go around and make people wet their pants and give up right away. Sure, cops have to pay out a bounty, but they have to do it anyway. Fucking actor playing at being a badass."

"You seriously believe that?"

"I know it's true."

James chuckled and shook his head. "You think my rep's

entirely bullshit? You haven't seen video of me doing takedowns?"

"Video? Fuck video. That shit was easy to fake even before all these elves and shit starting walking all over." Eddie reached into his pocket and pulled out some brass knuckles to slide onto his hand. His men did the same.

"You're making a mistake, asshole."

Eddie tapped his forehead. "Nah, I'm all about the truth and smart. You know I was telling people back in high school about how what most people think is bullshit. I did a report, you know, on pyramids, and how I knew it had to be aliens who built 'em."

"It wasn't aliens. It was Atlanteans."

James almost laughed. He wasn't sure if it was the beer or arrogance, but Eddie was a chatty guy. At least he hadn't opened fire.

Eddie shrugged. "Same fucking difference. The point is Brownstone, I can smell bullshit, and I smell it from you. No one man can be as tough as you. Taking out an entire gang by yourself? Fuck that. It's bullshit."

"I had a couple of people helping me with the Harriken toward the end." The bounty hunter shrugged. "So not just one man."

"Get a load of this fucker. He thinks he can mindfuck me." Eddie and his men laughed. "That's it, Brownstone. I'm done playing around. I'm gonna fucking beat you so badly that it'll take you six months to heal up, but I'm not gonna kill you. You see, after I fucking beat you down, I'm gonna get my phone out and record your broken-down ass and upload that to the internet for everyone to see so everyone knows that you're a lie." He pounded his chest. "I'm gonna be a fucking warrior of truth, you bullshit lie."

James gestured for them to come at him. "Less talk, more beat-down. Prove it, asshole."

Eddie snickered. "Stay here, guys. I'll handle this." He approached James with his fists raised and a smirk on his face.

The bounty hunter shook his head. This wouldn't even require the amulet. Pathetic.

The criminal finished his approach and threw a punch. James blocked it, but Eddie followed with a quick jab into his stomach.

James grunted and stumbled back.

Eddie grinned. "Yeah, I thought so. You're nothing but a name."

He threw another punch, but James dodged and grabbed his other arm as the criminal came in for the follow-up attack. James backhanded the criminal.

The bounty spun several times before hitting the ground.

"Don't piss me off, Eddie."

He hopped to his feet and wiped blood off his face, still grinning. "Okay, so you got a hit in. I'll give you that." He nodded to his men. "Brownstone wants us to take him seriously, so let's fucking take him seriously, boys."

The other two men advanced, and Eddie backed up to join them.

"You guys aren't even worth a quality beat-down," James rumbled. He slammed his fist into his palm. "And it's only because I'm not in a bad mood that I'm not kicking the shit out of you."

One of the men leaned down and grabbed a loose chunk from the parking lot. He pointed toward the F-350. "That old piece of shit is yours, isn't it? Everyone talks about how you drive some shit from twenty years ago."

James growled. "Fuck off."

All three men laughed. The level two hurled the chunk toward the F-350's windshield. It slammed into the truck and cracks spiderwebbed out from the point of impact.

James took several deep breaths, his hands clenching into fists. "I was trying to be nice about this shit." He stomped forward. "But you fuckers had to go and do something you should have never done."

Eddie snorted. "What the fuck? You mad because we hurt your stupid little piece-of-shit truck? I'll give you five dollars. That's how much it's worth."

James growled and charged. Eddie tried to get in a body blow, but the bounty hunter slammed a boot into the man's chest. The criminal's eyes widened as he traveled several yards before smashing into the ground. He groaned.

Another of the men swung his fist, and James grabbed his arm and yanked him forward. The thud of the savage follow-up headbutt was almost as loud as the crack of the chunk against his windshield. The man's eyes rolled up, and he fell to the ground.

The chunk-thrower leapt for James in a brave attempt at a tackle. The bounty hunter brought up his knee and the criminal hissed in pain at the contact.

James grabbed the man, not letting him fall to the ground. He smashed his fist into the man's face three quick times before tossing the battered and bleeding man to the ground.

"That's for my fucking truck, asshole. You're lucky I'm not killing your ass."

Eddie stumbled to his feet, his hand reaching into his coat.

James whipped out his .45 and fired. The bounty screamed as a bullet ripped into his arm. His gun fell to the ground and he followed, dropping to his knees and clutching his wounded arm.

Like an angry Michael ready to kick the Devil out of Heaven James marched toward Eddie, his baleful gaze fixed on the man. He holstered his gun before yanking the wounded criminal up by his collar.

"You know, asshole, sometimes reputations are there for a reason, and you're not the smartest fucker in the room."

Eddie spat blood in James' face. "Fuck you, Brownstone. I'm not begging."

Sirens sang in the distance.

James dropped the bounty to the ground. "Not gonna kill you, Eddie. You wouldn't be worth any money to me."

He kicked the man's chest, ribs cracking under the blow. Eddie's head bounced against the asphalt and he moaned, his eyes half-closed, and passed out.

James walked until he towered over the fallen man. "But I was sorely, *sorely* tempted to kill your ass, even with the money. Here's a tip, Eddie. Never, *ever* fuck with a man's truck."

18

An hour later, James stepped back into the Secret Sauce. Heather's son was asleep, his head on a table. Peaceful.

*Yeah, I helped protect that kid. Made some money doing it, but it's not a bad night's work. Wait, where's my barbeque?*

The bounty hunter frowned at the empty table. "I told you to not let them take my tray away. I know getting the bounties processed took a little longer than I would have liked, but I was looking forward to that food."

His stomach rumbled in protest.

The waiter from before emerged from the back a few seconds later with a fresh tray of barbequed pork. "Didn't want you eating something that had been sitting out for an hour." He set the tray on the table. "Don't worry, Mr. Brownstone. I called my boss and explained the situation, and he's fine with giving you another tray on the house."

James shrugged and sat. "Well, as long as I have more barbeque. Kicking those guy's asses worked up an appetite."

"Of course, Mr. Brownstone. If you need anything else, just let me know." The waiter disappeared into the back.

Heather stroked her sleeping son's hair and offered James a smile. "Sorry about the windshield on your truck."

"No biggie. The bounty from the guy who broke it was more than what the cost of repair will be. Just wish the fucker hadn't decided to do that. I tried to give them an out, but they had to keep pushing."

Heather nodded. "Yeah. I hacked cameras and had a drone up." She smiled. "Thanks for all this. I know they were bounties, but I also know that you didn't have to do this. It's not like anyone makes James Brownstone do anything he doesn't want to do."

*Well, no one who isn't named Shay.*

James shook his head. "If they were sniffing around you because of shit you did for me it's my responsibility." He ripped some delicious pork flesh off a rib and swallowed. "Here's the thing... This has got me thinking. I know a little something about people hiding from their past."

"Oh?"

"Yeah. Not something I've had to worry about, but I've got some close...friends who have. I also know the more you try to hide, the more power people have over you. You need to take back your life, Heather."

The hacker rolled her eyes. "No offense, James, but you're a class-six bounty hunter and your soon-to-be adopted daughter is safe behind the walls of a government magic school."

James stared at her for a moment, surprised she knew that much about Alison.

"Yeah, that's right. I know your deal. It's not like I didn't check you out thoroughly." Heather shrugged. "The point is, I have to be on the move to be safe, and I'm not able to defend myself like you are. I mean, you just punted a few grown men around like they were ragdolls."

"No, you *don't* have to move all the time." James shook his head. "You just need to be somewhere that people know it's not a smart move to attack, or at least a place where it makes them pause and think first. Kind of like Alison and the School of Necessary Magic."

"Well, my son isn't magical and neither am I." Heather sighed. "So I don't know what to do."

"I've got a solution. I think we should talk about you being properly employed."

"Properly employed?"

James nodded and swallowed another bite of barbeque. "Yeah, employed by me, as my personal computer assistant or support person or whatever shit you want to call it. Full-time. I can pay you through the Brownstone Agency, or we can arrange something else. You get some steady money that'll help you and your son, and I can use your help with tough jobs like Schwartz. If I've learned anything in this last year, it's that even *I* can't take everyone on by myself, and to get experts to help me with my weak spots."

"Get help? Like you said about the Harriken?"

The bounty hunter grinned. "Yeah. Had the help of other people, not just the cops."

Heather sighed. "Not saying I'm not interested, but paying me money doesn't solve my safety problem."

"It does if you move to LA. I can have your back right away instead of having to drive six hours to help you."

James set his rib down and glanced between another rib and some brisket. He decided on the brisket.

A few bites later he offered, "Move to my neighborhood. Between the cops and the locals it might not be the nicest-looking place, but it's safe, and getting safer by the day. Can't judge it by its appearance."

"I know. It's not the most expensive place, despite your money. It's one of the reasons I like you. You aren't pretentious." Heather looked down. "I'm not so sure about that. How do you know there's a place I can even stay there? A place that would be good for my son and me."

James grunted. "I know a place. Not only a good place, but a super-fucking-safe place."

"Where? And why is it safe?"

"Because it's an apartment owned by cop who is known to be a close personal friend of mine. Sergeant Mack of the LAPD. There's also a good Magnet school in the area, and I'm sure having a cop vouch for you will help your kid get in when it's time for him to start school."

Heather's expression alternated between hope and confusion. "You want me to live with a cop as my landlord? You do know I've done a lot of illegal stuff? Hell, I've done illegal stuff for you."

"Hey, if you're working for me, Mack will have no problem with you." James shrugged, not sure what else to say. "Your call. You're a good asset, and I need someone like you. But I'm not gonna force you. I can only offer you money and some protection."

"I'll think about it. That's all I can promise."

"Fair enough." James took another bite of his brisket. "I'm gonna polish off the rest of this barbeque, then I'm gonna find a place to stay for the night." He shook his head. "Six hours to LA? California is too damned big."

Heather laughed.

---

Sergeant Choi tapped on his keyboard behind the front counter and shook his head. "Damn, Trey. You guys went on a tear this time. Keep this up, and there won't be many bounties left in Vegas." He chuckled.

Trey leaned against the counter with a smirk on his face. "That's how the Brownstone Agency rolls, Sergeant. Why waste time and let bounties run around doing what they want?"

"Just surprised at some of these. I mean, I'm glad you brought in Jacob Johns, but I'd heard he hired a witch bodyguard. You guys are good, but I thought that'd be more a Brownstone thing than a Brownstone Agency thing."

Trey snorted. "Please, Sergeant. The Brownstone Agency ain't afraid of a few witches. Los Angeles is crawling with that sort of shit. We're ready to take on whatever we need to get our man, just like our boss."

The sergeant looked around for a moment and then leaned in closer. "I want you to level with me."

"About what?"

"It's not like we don't know about your background."

Trey narrowed his eyes. He wondered if some thug disrespect was coming his way. It was a good thing Shorty and the rest of the boys were back at the loft with his aunt. They wouldn't be able to handle disrespect from a cop.

"What about my background?"

The cop shrugged. "It's not every day that a bunch of gang members decide to put on suits and switch teams."

"And what do you think about that, Sergeant?" Trey tried to keep the hostility out of his voice.

"I'm not complaining. You guys are taking down bounties left and right, and you're doing it with a lot more professionalism than a lot of guys running around calling themselves bounty hunters. It's not what I would have expected, but I guess it makes sense to apply street smarts to bounty hunting." Sergeant Choi frowned. "I don't know. The average gang member around here doesn't strike me as the type who would want to get a bounty-hunting license and start running down their fellow criminals." He entered a few more lines into the bounty-processing document he was working on.

Trey snorted. "You see, that's where you're all twisted up about this."

"How?"

The bounty hunter nodded down the hallway to where a frowning and handcuffed man with a black eye was being led to the lock-up by an officer. "Why do you think I joined a gang to begin with? Why do you think I worked my way up to lead the gang?"

"I don't know, you liked power? Kicking ass? You wanted people to be afraid of you?"

Trey shook his head. "My nana always wanted the best for me. She looked after me when I didn't have a mom around to keep an eye on me. She's a good woman; goes to church, worked her entire life. But that didn't stop bullets from passing through her living room because some dumbasses were doing a drive-by in the neigh-borhood."

Sergeant Choi stopped typing and focused on Trey.

"Yeah, I wanted power and for people to be afraid," the bounty hunter continued. "I wanted people to be so fucking afraid they wouldn't dare fuck with anyone I cared about or even think about letting bullets fly without my permission." Trey slammed his hand down on the counter. "That's what most gangs are, Sergeant. You're a cop; you've got to know that. It's about protection in places where you can't always depend on anyone else."

The cop and the bounty hunter silently locked eyes for a long moment.

"Do you feel safe now in your neighborhood?" Sergeant Choi asked. "Even though you aren't in a gang anymore?"

"You're wrong. I'm still in a gang. I'm just in a tougher fucking gang." Trey ran his hand down his lapel. "This is a uniform. These are gang colors for the Brownstone Agency, led by the toughest motherfucker in the United States; a man who is so strong he brought down the Harriken." He shook his head. "I don't need to be in charge, Sergeant. All I ever wanted was for my nana and friends to be safe, and now Mr. Brownstone's shown me how I can do that and not annoy the 5-0. He started by giving me respect, and I gave him respect back."

Sergeant Choi held his hands in front of him. "No disrespect was meant, Trey. I'm really happy with how you guys are performing. I was just curious."

"No problem, Sergeant. I'm just happy the Brownstone Agency can be of assistance to the great city of Las Vegas."

"You guys are a huge help. I know your teams rotate

and are part-time, but I'm hoping someday that we'll get a permanent branch office here in Vegas."

Trey shrugged. "Never know what the future will bring."

"Okay, just let me finish these documents, and it'll free up the funds due."

"Always nice doing business with you, Sergeant."

19

James smiled. His exit was coming up, and he'd be back home soon. He wasn't sure what Heather would decide about working for him or moving to Los Angeles, but taking down Eddie Green hadn't been a mistake.

*Fucking asshole should have just surrendered. People ask for my picture in restaurants, but there's always some fucker who thinks I'm all talk and no walk.*

He frowned as he took in the crack on his windshield. He'd need to get that taken care of soon. Without any bounties coming up, he should have time to get it taken care of that day.

*And those fuckers really, really shouldn't have hurt my truck.*

Beating a man to a pulp because he damaged your truck wasn't an overreaction. It was justice.

The bounty hunter's hands tightened around his steering wheel. A loose piece of pavement to the windshield wasn't as bad as wood smashing into his truck from his burning house, but his poor F-350 had been through a lot in the last year.

*I wonder if Zoe knows someone who could make some sort of potion for my truck. Maybe even her. Is that even a thing? Maybe I could apply it like wax or some shit.*

James' phone rang, snapping him out of his truck-related brooding. He shook his head and glanced down at his phone on the console. Tyler was calling, so the bounty hunter answered on speakerphone.

"What's up, Tyler?"

"Lars Hansen just called," Tyler explained. "He's ready for the party to begin."

James pulled from his lane into his exit. "He's got the time?"

"Yeah. He says he wants the showdown to be in four hours."

"What? four hours from right now?" James grunted and turned off the exit onto a surface street.

"Of course. What do you think it'd be, four hours from next Tuesday?"

James' many conversations with Alison had trained him well. He could hear Tyler's eyes roll.

The bounty hunter grunted. "You're lucky I just got back to town."

"Wait, you weren't in town? Brownstone, you had this fight coming up. What the fuck were you doing?"

"Bounty hunting, asshole. I'm not your fucking employee."

*Shit. Why did I even agree to this?*

Tyler muttered something under his breath. "Just

saying, this might be your one shot to get this guy without him being in the middle of a park or something."

James didn't respond to Tyler immediately. Instead, he took a hard turn into a nearby parking lot before pulling out again and heading back toward the onramp. He hated that Tyler was right.

"Don't whine about it," the bounty hunter rumbled. "I'm back now. I'll grab some gas on the edge of town, get some gear, and then head straight to the fucking Salton Sea."

Tyler let out a sigh of relief. "Good. For a second there, I thought you were going to flake on me."

"Nah. I've got an appointment with a level five."

*Fucking Lars. You couldn't give me a day's notice?*

---

Tyler whistled to himself as he counted money at his desk in his back office. Betting on Brownstone might be uncomfortable, but winning was a foregone conclusion with the man's track record. At least this time he wasn't alone. There was a healthy pro-Brownstone betting faction, even among people who otherwise hated the bounty hunter.

*Some of these idiots can actually learn. Good for them. Can't run away from the truth, no matter how annoying it is.*

The information broker's greed murdered his earlier concern over helping his nemesis. If Tyler ever got upset later that he was working with Brownstone, he figured he'd just go to the bank, withdraw a pile of hundred-dollar bills, and roll around in it.

*I've got to stop thinking like a short-sighted idiot and*

*remember that I'm a successful businessman. Brownstone's not my partner. He's a product I'm exploiting to make money.*

*Maybe I'll even start another place in a different spot in town. Kathy can run it, and collect more info for me. Yeah, that shit would work out well.*

Tyler stood and moved to the corner of the room. He placed his palm over a smooth spot on the wall. A light flashed, and a hidden panel popped open to reveal a safe.

He tapped in a code to open the safe and slipped the money inside.

"Thanks, Brownstone, for making me the money to pay for this safe and the palm reader. Maybe I'll upgrade to a DNA scanner with what I win from this fight." He rubbed his chin. If he made enough money, he could start messing around with trying to get some magical protection.

*Brownstone obviously uses a lot of magic. At least potions, but I bet he's got all sorts of artifacts hidden on him when he fights. Doesn't matter, as long as it makes me money.*

Tyler laughed. Nothing like being a winner no matter what.

He closed the safe and the hidden panel. Between online and physical bets, he was going to make a shit-ton of money just off his take from the pot, let alone what he'd earned off Brownstone's victory.

*Maybe I should hedge against him. It's not like Brownstone will always win. He's just a guy, not a god.*

Someone knocked on his door.

"What?"

The door opened, and Kathy stepped through. "A large blond asshole is here to see you."

"Lars Hansen?"

She nodded. "Yeah. I can't believe you told that guy to come here. He smells of trouble."

"Of course he does. That's why I'm going to make money." Tyler walked toward the door. "The man wanted to place some bets, and I want his money. Don't worry, this situation is completely under control."

Kathy rolled her eyes. "You think that throwing some level five at Brownstone and being involved directly in that shit is having the situation completely under control?" The woman shook her head. "For such a smart guy, Tyler, sometimes you can be a real dumbass."

Tyler stopped at the door and frowned. "Okay, Miz Junior Bartender and Info Broker, explain to me how this is a problem? I'm making money, and both Brownstone and Lars know the score. The cops can't bitch about Brownstone going after a bounty, and it's not like I'm setting him up, because he agreed to the whole thing." He shrugged. "Is this just you being a chick?"

"Being a chick?"

"Yeah, you know—soft."

Kathy snorted and spun on her heel. "Whatever. Your place. I just work here."

Tyler followed her down the hallway to the main room. She led him straight to Lars Hansen. With a slight bow, she mockingly gestured to the huge criminal before making her way behind the bar.

Seeing a picture of Lars Hansen didn't have the impact of staring at the behemoth from only a yard away. The level five glowered down at Tyler. His thick muscles strained his wifebeater, and an arrogant smirk covered his face.

*Yeah, here's a guy who thinks he's going to win. Good. I can use that.*

Tyler looked to either side of the man. A skinny redheaded man in a trench coat stood to Lars' side, but the info broker knew not to judge him on his appearance.

It was Patrick Cavanaugh. The level-four wizard might not be as strong as Lars, but he could blow shit up well enough with his wand.

Tyler narrowed his eyes. Patrick had turned Tyler's offer down. He didn't recognize the dangerous-looking dark-haired man on Lars' other side, but he suspected he was another level four or five who'd been too chickenshit to take the information broker's offer.

He didn't understand what they were doing there. Maybe they wanted in on the betting action, even if they were too afraid to participate themselves?

*Wait, this could work. If Brownstone doesn't kill Lars, maybe some of the other guys would be at least willing to try. But what if they do kill Brownstone?*

Tyler furrowed his brow and rubbed his chin. If he couldn't get another bounty hunter, maybe he could arrange some sort of high-end fight club between criminals. He'd have to wait and see how the first match went before he worried about future business opportunities.

Lars yanked out a wad of bills from his pants pocket. "All on me for the kill, Tyler." He held out the money. "Unless you know something about Brownstone I don't."

Tyler took the money. "Nope. It's not exactly like his ass-kicking is secret, though. You, though, got a nice ability. You're not some wizard that Brownstone can smash in the face and win." Tyler risked a quick glance at Patrick.

The wizard's mouth pressed into a thin line, but he didn't say anything.

*You're the pussy who didn't agree to the fight.*

Lars grunted. "Yeah. Brownstone's just a man, and I've taken out entire teams before. That fucker is going down."

Tyler started counting the money. "You don't want to bet using any of the other categories? All sorts of nice categories here. If you're confident, you can even make money by directing the fight. You know, maybe just maiming Brownstone instead of killing him? It's more profitable odds, since everyone expects this fight to end in a kill."

"Fuck that. All I need to do is kill Brownstone and make money off it."

Lars' flunkies chuckled.

*Patrick, you fucking pussy. You're acting all tough now, but you couldn't be bothered to be a headliner like Lars.*

Tyler forced a smile on his face. "What about you, Patrick? You want to place a bet?" He glanced at Lars' second friend. "Or maybe this guy?"

"Victor," the man offered. His voice had a slight Russian accent. "I'll bet on Brownstone dying."

*Victor? Fuck, I called that asshole, too, and he blew me off.*

Patrick nodded. "Yeah. I'll bet on Brownstone dying."

Tyler accepted their money and nodded. "You all seem pretty confident that your boy Lars is going to be able to take it."

The three men all smirked at the same time. It tightened Tyler's stomach.

Lars shrugged. "Not gambling if you know you're gonna win."

*What the fuck? Something's wrong here.*

Two more large men pushed into the Black Sun and walked toward the trio.

Lars gave them a slight nod. "You two watch this place. Make sure the bookie keeps taking bets, but also make sure he doesn't ruin it for us."

Tyler frowned. "What the hell is that supposed to mean?"

"It means, loser, that you didn't set any rules." Lars lifted his hand. The skin grayed and hardened. "All I agreed to is to show up at specific coordinates." He laughed. "You didn't say I couldn't bring friends."

The room fell silent as everyone inside the Black Sun focused their attention on Tyler and Lars.

Tyler kept a smile painted on his face to hide the panic that sent his heart thundering. "Yeah, I guess I *didn't* say anything about that."

Lars stepped toward the info broker until he towered over the other man. "You talk a good game about being neutral, but what's that even mean? It means you're working with the cops, and you're the one who was calling around on Brownstone's behalf."

"I'm just trying to make some money here, Lars. I'm not on anyone's side."

The level five gave Tyler a feral grin. "Good, then you won't mind if my two new friends keep an eye on you. If you try to let Brownstone know about this shit we'll have to have a little discussion, fucker."

"Wait one second. The Black Sun is neutral ground."

Lars snorted and shrugged. "Don't see any cops here right now, fucker." He flipped Tyler off and headed toward the door, trailed by Patrick and Victor.

Tyler sighed and walked over to the odds board. "Because of the new information, the odds have changed. Give me a few minutes to update everything."

*Fuck. Do I tell Brownstone? This is bullshit. He'll think I set him up.*

He started erasing the info in some of the boxes, his face tight. Even ignoring Brownstone, Tyler didn't like thugs hanging on him and threatening him in the Black Sun. There were no cops here and they likely wouldn't do anything unless actual violence broke out, but if he let these assholes intimidate him, everything he'd built up with the Black Sun would be worth nothing.

A man just couldn't tolerate disrespect in his own place.

2 0

James had just finished fueling up when his stomach rumbled. He grunted. He needed to eat, but he didn't have time to grab some good barbeque. He hopped into the F-350 and brought the truck to life.

Fuel. Just like his F-350, the bounty hunter needed a lot of fuel for his upcoming Lars ass-kicking. He'd already stopped by his warehouse to grab a few goodies, but he hadn't thought to get anything to eat.

James pulled out of the gas station and frowned. He was already hungry, so driving another couple of hours would leave him ravenous.

"Fuck. Why does driving always make me twice as hungry? All I'm doing is sitting here."

A yellow and red sign down the road caught his attention. In-N-Out Burger. Not barbeque, but it'd do.

James pulled into the drive-thru and waited behind the long line of cars. In a moment he pulled up to a cheerful teen holding a tablet. "Welcome to In-N-Out Burger, sir. May I take your order?"

"I read online the other day that you can order a Quad Quad from the Not-So-Secret Menu. Is that true?"

"Yes, sir. You want a Quad Quad?"

James shook his head. "No, I want three Quad Quads."

The girl blinked. "Three? Sir, just so you understand, that's twelve patties."

"Yeah, you're right. I'll take four Quad Quads. So you know, a quad of Quad Quads."

"Your stomach." She smiled, tapped at her screen, and walked to the next car in line.

*That should be enough fuel to kick Lars' ass.*

---

Tyler and Kathy sat in front of the odds board next to a table with a small lockbox on top. A crowd of scumbags surrounded them. Many of the men were waving their cash in front of them or above their heads, shouting out their bets, desperate and worried the fight would start before they could get their money down. They feared missing out on the fight of the decade, if not the century.

"One thousand on Lars," shouted a suited man with slicked-back hair.

A massive biker shoved him out of the way. "Two thousand on Lars, though I also want to put five hundred dollars down on maiming."

"Single-file line, please," Kathy called. "Everyone calm down. We still have time. Brownstone's not even there yet."

Tyler surveyed the huge crowd, his heart pounding, his jaw clenched.

*Shit. The bets aren't balanced enough. The odds are way in*

*Lars' favor, but I don't know if I have enough to cover all these bets if Brownstone loses. Fuck. If I welch on a bet, my neutrality won't mean shit.*

Tyler did his best to keep a smile on his face, especially when Lars' two goons looked his way.

*Need to find out a way to level this out. Warning Brownstone would be one way.*

His phone chimed with alerts of more online bets, but it was in the hand of one of Lars' goons. The smirking man held it up to taunt Tyler.

*Need to get my phone back so I can at least warn Brownstone. At this rate, not only is he going to get killed, I'm going go broke—or people are going to break me when I can't pay them.*

Tyler frowned.

*Maybe there's a different way to work this. Got to use my assets, like my mind. Stop thinking like a thug like Brownstone or Lars.*

"Great money-making opportunity if you bet on Brownstone," the information broker yelled. "You can be rich. At this point, betting on Lars is like putting your money in some savings account. Why not take the longer odds? Bigger risk, bigger reward. Now, that's what I call gambling. That's what a real man does."

A man scoffed and slammed his fist on the table. "Fuck that. Brownstone's not gonna be able to take out Lars, Patrick, and Victor together. Why should I throw my money away? So you can profit, you little piece-of-shit rat?"

Several other people shouted in agreement.

*Oh, you fuckers. You think you can disrespect me in my own place? I'll remember everyone one of you assholes. If Brownstone comes out on top, maybe I'll use my winnings to hire some badass magical thugs as security here. Can't always depend on the cops.*

He glanced around. There wasn't a single cop in the place.

Tyler gave the man a grin and shrugged. "Just trying to make you all some money. Don't have to be an asshole about it."

The man yanked the information broker up by the collar of his shirt. "You calling me an asshole, you piece of shit?"

Tyler gave him a defiant stare. "The Black Sun is neutral ground. You want to hit me, fine, but you're going to lose that neutral status. Then you'll have to deal with the cops and you won't have access to shit like this Brown-stone vs. Lars match, so I would think long and hard about what you want to do. A few seconds of fun isn't worth the trouble."

The man released Tyler and snorted. "You're right. You're not worth it." He returned to the crowd.

Tyler smoothed down his shirt and vest before returning to his seat. "Thought so."

Kathy leaned over to whisper, "You've fucked this shit up badly. I hope you realize that. We're lucky that's the worst thing that has happened."

"This isn't done," Tyler whispered back. "A good businessman takes advantage of opportunities as they pop up, and I still have plenty of chances to salvage this shit. A few hotheads aren't going to cost me a big payday." He tapped his nose. "I know how to smell a profit."

Katy snorted and straightened. "Whatever."

James was on his third Quad Quad when Heather called. He set his burger in its wrapper next to the bag on the passenger seat before answering on speakerphone.

"Think over my offer?" the bounty hunter inquired. "I can give you Sergeant Mack's number so you can talk about renting his place."

"I'm still thinking about that, but that's not what this is about."

"What? Did taking Eddie out not solve your problem?"

James frowned and switched lanes to pass. The I-10 East was surprisingly packed, but at least traffic was flowing at a reasonable pace. He didn't want to be late for his beat-down.

"No," Heather answered. "Eddie's merc hacker stopped looking, just like I thought he would. It's just I've been keeping an eye on some stuff related to you, including odds for some sort of fight you're supposed to have with a bounty. There's a massive amount of betting activity centered at the Black Sun. What the hell is that about?"

James grunted. "Found out about that? It's not a fight, it's a bounty capture. Tyler has criminal contacts, and he convinced a bounty to face me at a scheduled time. I picked the place, the Salton Sea, where I know I can go all-out and not worry about innocent people getting hurt."

"So, what, you're some sort of fighter now? Going to move to Vegas and get in the ring?"

"No. I'd have to go after the bounty anyway. This way I don't have to go looking, and I can make some more money on the side."

Heather sighed. "Whatever. I'm a hacker, not a bounty hunter, but I do know that the odds went from favoring you to heavily favoring the other guy. There's some talk on the dark web too about this. Everyone's saying you're going to get killed, and it'll be the end of the 'Brownstone Reign of Terror.'"

"They wish." James pulled in behind an eighteen-wheeler and briefly imagined what it'd be like to have one to haul a massive barbeque pit. "It's just a bunch of scumbags convincing themselves of bullshit. I'm used to that kind of thing. It's not a big deal."

"I do understand a little something about money. Even scumbags don't like to just give up their money unless they have a good reason to." The sound of her tapping at her keyboard came over the line. "I've got a feed from the Black Sun now, and everyone's really spun up. They are practically throwing money down to bet. Don't have any audio, though, so can't tell you what they are saying."

James snorted. "Knowing that asshole Tyler, he's probably just conned them all with some bullshit so he can make more money off betting. Maybe he told them how I was out of town and might be late so the odds would shift and he could win more betting on me."

"Wait, Tyler's going to bet on you?"

"Yeah. Every time he does he makes a lot of money, so he's learned his fucking lesson. Don't bet against James Brownstone in a fight."

Heather's breath caught.

James frowned. "What is it?"

"Nothing. I just thought someone was going to kick Tyler's ass, but they backed off."

The bounty hunter grunted. To his surprise, the idea of some asshole beating Tyler down didn't bring the smile he'd expected to his face.

"Huh," Heather commented. "Oh, I wonder if this will change anything."

"What now?" James glanced at his In-N-Out bag. He wanted to know what was going on, but he also wanted to finish eating before his burgers got cold.

"That AET lieutenant…you know, Hall? She just walked in."

"She's got a weird schedule, so it's not strange she'd be there in the day." James reached over to grab the burger. He could sneak bites in during the conversation. "Remember, Tyler's neutrality shit only works because he's got AET helping to enforce it."

"He might have some trouble with that soon."

James gobbled down a delicious bite of cheese and ground beef. "Why?"

"She looks kind of pissed."

---

Maria frowned and surveyed the bar. The Black Sun could be boisterous at times with all the scum that frequented the place, but this near-riot surprised her.

Her neck muscles tightened, and her heart sped up. Every cop instinct in her was screaming that something was wrong. Very wrong.

She grabbed her badge from her belt and slipped it into her pocket. It was a good thing she wasn't in uniform.

Maria crept around the edge of the shouting crowd

surrounding Tyler and Kathy at a table. An odds board sat next to them.

*That can mean only one thing. Something is up with Brownstone. What has that dumbass gotten himself into now? Waging war on all the Triads in California now, or the Russian Mafia? Did he issue a challenge to the Drow to return?*

The frowning lieutenant maneuvered through the crowd until she was only a few yards from Tyler. Men waved money and shouted around her.

"I need to place my bet," a Demon General yelled from right in front of her. "Fuck Brownstone. I'm putting five hundred on Lars."

Maria tapped the man on his shoulder. The gangbanger spun around with murder in his eyes until he spotted who'd tapped him. She might not be as famous as Brownstone, but she came to the Black Sun often enough.

"I ain't do no shit here at the Black Sun. You can't touch me. That's the rules. That's *your* rules, cop."

Maria rolled her eyes. "I don't even know who the fuck you are, so, yeah, I'm not interested in arresting you." She pointed at the board. "What the fuck is going on?"

"Ain't you heard? I thought you would know because you've bet on this shit before. Brownstone's taking on Lars Hansen."

The cop's hands curled into fists. "Lars Hansen, the level five? The cop killer? The AET killer?"

The gang member laughed. "Yeah, bitch. That dude, but it's some weird shit. Tyler he got Lars to agree to meet Brownstone at the Salton Sea at a certain time, so it's more like an MMA fight than bounty shit."

*Fucking Brownstone. What was your brilliant plan? Keep*

*him away from the city? Stop always trying to be such a fucking martyr. Last time you almost got your ass killed.*

Maria sighed. She'd hoped the bounty hunter would have learned to trust AET a little more after their recent interactions, but they obviously had a long way to go.

Tyler glanced at her and jumped up from his chair. "That's right, everyone," he yelled. The boisterous crowd grew quiet. "The odds are against the famous James Brownstone, because Lars Hansen, being a cowardly piece of shit, is bringing two other people, both levels fours, to gang up on Brownstone. Now, *I* would have been far more interested in a straight-forward fight, but there's still money to be made in the Great Brownstone Ambush if you act now."

Two large men who'd been lounging near the bar shoved their way through the crowd and stomped over toward Tyler.

"What did you just say about Lars?" one of the men growled.

"Just explaining the situation."

The man shoved Tyler. "No, you said he was a cowardly piece of shit."

Tyler shrugged. "Hey, he's obviously afraid, which is why he needed to bring help to take down Brownstone. I'm just disappointed, is all. I thought the great Lars Hansen wouldn't need help, but instead, he had to go and cry and say he needed backup. How is that not cowardly? It'd be like Brownstone calling for surprise help."

The thug slammed a fist into Tyler's stomach. The information broker doubled over and fell to his knees, coughing and groaning.

A roar went up from the crowd. Several people complained about their bets not being taken.

"Fuck, that hurt," Tyler wheezed. "You sonofabitch."

Kathy gasped and scrambled out of her seat. "You can't do that. It's against the rules."

Tyler's assailant sneered. "Fuck you, bitch, and fuck your boss. *My* boss told me to make sure that Tyler didn't try any shit, and I think being disrespectful is trying shit."

Maria shook her head. She reached into her back pocket instead of her jacket. A gunfight in a crowded bar would result in too much collateral damage, but she still had surprise on her side. She grabbed a small silver telescoping baton from her pocket and pulled it out. With a quick thrust, it snapped to full length.

The Demon General grinned at her. "Can I join in, too, cop? Come on. That was a bitch move, sucker-punching Tyler."

She shook her head. "Stay out of it. It's cop business now."

"You're no fun."

"Nope."

Maria raised the baton and advanced on the two thugs standing over Tyler.

He looked up from the ground and flipped off the thug. One of the thugs slugged him, and Tyler slammed to the ground.

He wiped some blood from his mouth and grinned. "You just lost your neutrality, asshole."

21

Maria continued advancing on the thug, her weapon in hand. Another man joined him to kick Tyler.

*It's been a while since I had to remind people why this place is neutral. Disrespecting the neutrality here means disrespecting the AET, and it's important that these assholes remember who is in charge.*

The thug glanced her way, his gaze dropping to her baton. "You got a problem, bitch?"

Maria pointed her baton at Tyler. "You're assaulting the owner of this place. You can't honestly expect me to stand by and let that happen."

The man snorted. "You want some of this too? Maybe we can offer you a little rod after we're done with Tyler."

His friend grinned, feral hunger in his eyes.

*Cocky assholes. Good. If they had powers, they would have already used them. They shouldn't be a problem.*

"Leave right now." Maria raised the baton. "I don't want trouble here. That's the whole damned point of the neutrality. Why don't you and your friend just walk away?

You can tell everyone how you kicked Tyler's ass and laugh about it."

The first thug squared his shoulders. "You think I'm afraid of some bitch?"

"I'm not just some bitch. I'm a cop with AET."

"So what? I run with Lars Hansen. He's killed plenty of cops and AET."

Maria nodded and looked him up and down. "You're just his errand boy, I'm guessing. I don't recognize you, which means you're not a level four or higher. I don't need armor and a rifle to take your ass down."

He frowned. "Fuck you, bitch. You think I'm afraid to beat a cop down?"

"Three-to-one Maria kicks their asses," Tyler croaked.

The man silenced him with a kick. "Shut your mouth, fucker, if you want to be alive at the end of this." He looked at his partner. "Three to one? More like ten to one." He laughed.

Several men rushed toward the table to slap down bets, and the thug stopped laughing. The men placing bets hurried back into the crowd, allowing a circle of space in the center.

The thug narrowed his eyes at the cop. "You should have been the one to walk away, bitch. Now you're gonna pay."

*Still too many people to use my gun. Need to rattle his cage a little so I have the advantage.*

Maria sneered. "You're an idiot, which is why you're here instead of helping take down Brownstone."

"You're dead, bitch."

With a grunt, the man lunged. The cop spun, dodging

his grasp. Two quick strikes to his knees with the baton had him on the ground groaning. A nice kick to the head with her boot sent him to the Land of Nod.

"My name isn't 'bitch,' it's Maria." She kicked him again.

His partner yanked out a knife. "I'm gonna carve you up good."

Maria snorted. "You're seriously trying to intimidate me with a knife? Give me a fucking break. I've stared down demons and portals to other worlds, you dumb piece of shit."

The man swiped at her, and she blocked his strike with her baton. She backed off, glancing to either side to make sure no one was planning to join in, but everyone was just watching and cheering as if they were at a boxing match.

*Need to end this quickly.*

The cop sprinted forward when the thug bumped into a table and smashed his wrist with the baton. He yelled, and his knife clattered to the ground.

Maria followed up with a knee in his groin. The man howled in pain and bent over. A quick blow to the head sent him to the ground, moaning.

"Damn!" shouted the gang member from earlier. "She laid those bitches out like they were nothing."

The cop sighed and knelt by the second man.

"You...*bitch*," he moaned.

"I already told you. Not bitch, asshole." Maria collapsed her baton and stuck it back in her pocket. "Lieutenant Maria Hall, AET."

A murmur rippled through the crowd as two uniformed officers pushed their way through. They stopped when they hit the clear circle where the thugs had met their fate.

One of the cops looked down at the men on the ground. "We got a call about an assault in progress. Weren't sure if we should come because of the whole neutrality thing, Lieutenant." He frowned.

*Don't give a shit if you approve. Only give a shit if you have my back as a fellow cop.*

Maria nudged her second victim with her foot. "These guys were beating on the owner of the place. They refused to leave, so it was necessary for me to take them down."

"We'll take it from here, Lieutenant." The cop fished out handcuffs and shook his head. "Stupid idiots."

Maria marched over to Tyler, who had relocated to a chair at this point and was holding his stomach. His face was swollen and he'd have an obvious black eye soon, but he seemed otherwise okay.

She eyed him in silence, wondering if he'd been purposely trying to get the men to hit him so she could take care of them, or even as a warning that Brownstone was in danger.

*He can't honestly care, can he?*

It didn't matter. She needed him to clarify a few things so she knew how angry she should be with him.

Maria pointed toward the hallway. "I need to talk to you, Tyler. Now."

He shook his head. "I've got bets to take, and I've got to pay out for the bets on you. Money goes before comfort."

Maria rolled her eyes. "This isn't about comfort, and it wasn't a request."

Kathy stepped away from the edge of the crowd. "I can handle the bets, Tyler."

The cop grabbed Tyler's arm and yanked him out of the chair. "Come on, before I get really pissed and finish what they started."

The info broker muttered under his breath as the AET lieutenant dragged him into the hallway and away from the crowd.

The cop took a deep breath. "Before I had to save your ass from those two thugs, I had an interesting conversation with a chatty gang member. I'm hoping he was confused, because if he's not, you and Brownstone conspired to set up some sort of fight event in the Salton Sea with a level-five bounty, and you didn't mention any of this to me or anyone else in the department. I'm also really having trouble believing this because it involves you working closely with Brownstone."

Tyler shrugged, then winced a little and leaned against the wall. "I made such a persuasive case that even that thug Brownstone realized it was a good idea. Except…things have gotten complicated."

"Because Lars is now going to ambush Brownstone with two other guys."

Tyler nodded and offered her a pained smile. "Yeah, that's kind of how it worked out. It wasn't exactly the plan, but it's how things ended."

"And Tweedledee and Tweedledum in the bar? What was their deal?"

"Some of Lars' guys. They didn't want me warning Brownstone. I figured that even if they kicked the shit out of me, you'd be able to get a warning to him. They had my phone." He frowned. "I need to remember to go grab it. Maybe Kathy did."

Maria stared at him. "*You* wanted to warn Brownstone?"

Tyler waved a hand. "Don't get me wrong. This isn't about saving his ass. I've just got a lot of money riding on him."

Maria groaned and scrubbed a hand over her face. "You stupid fucking moron. No, I should say, you stupid fucking morons. What? Did you honestly think some piece of shit cop-killer would play nice? That you could control him?"

"Um, yes?"

She jabbed a finger in his chest. "You know what? This is the problem with men. You can't think past your dicks. I would have thought Brownstone would have been too stubborn for this sort of shit, and you too smart." She spun on her heel. "I don't know if I'll be able to get AET there in time to save him."

"Brownstone knew what he was agreeing to. Uh, mostly. It's not your problem."

Maria stormed off. "Call Brownstone. Warn him. At least he'll have a fucking chance then."

Tyler followed along. "Look, mistakes happen."

She continued pushing her way through the crowd toward the entrance.

"The time's almost up," Tyler shouted to the crowd. "Place your final bets, and all you assholes who bet on those three dicks when I was getting my ass kicked? Those count!"

Shay stomped back and forth, kicking at the dust and rocks, her heart thundering. She glared at the surrounding pine trees, clutching her phone.

She wanted to punch someone. A tree would have to do.

*James, you stupid fucking idiot. You purposely kept* this *from me, too.*

The tomb raider took several deep breaths and slowly let them out. There was nothing she could do about James. She wasn't in a city, so even if Peyton could find a wizard or she could stumble on some hidden magical passage, it didn't matter. James would have to win the battle on his own. Just like with the Drow, by the time she got there it'd be too late.

She dialed Alison. The girl deserved to know what was going on, and what might happen.

*You better not die, James. You'll break that poor girl's heart.*

"Hey, Mo...Aunt Shay," Alison answered.

"Stupid fucking idiot men with shit moronic actions," Shay shouted into the phone. "I fucking hate them all!"

"Um, excuse me?"

Shay kicked a nearby dried stump. "Your dad is a fucking moron, and the next time I see him, I'm gonna strangle him. Then I'm gonna shoot him. Then I'm gonna bring him back to life so I can throw him off a building."

"O-okay. Are you all right, Aunt Shay? Did you have some sort of fight? I mean, I know Dad's still working on the whole emotional intelligence thing, but this is a little mean, I think."

The tomb raider resisted throwing her phone to the

ground and stomping on it. It wasn't Alison's fault. Or the phone's.

"Your *idiot* dad decided he was gonna set up some sort of scheduled bounty capture and make money off it. Kind of like a pay-per-view fight. But because he's a bounty hunter and not a girl who can see souls or a super-smart tomb raider who can see through bullshit, he didn't anticipate that he might get tricked. So now he's walking straight into an ambush of a level-five guy and two level-fours when he thinks it's just gonna be one guy. Stupid pig-fucking-headed moron."

Alison sighed. "This is Dad we're talking about. Even if there are extra tough guys, I'm sure he can handle it. He's always been able to before."

Shay threw up a hand. "There's nothing I can do about it either. I'm seriously in the middle of nowhere, and I have absolutely no way of getting there in time. I'm extra fucking pissed, too, because I asked him the other day if he was up to anything, and he conveniently forgot to mention all this. That proves it. That fucking *proves* that he knew this was bullshit."

"Aunt Shay, you need to take a few deep breaths and calm down. Getting really worked up about it won't help, and if worse comes to worst, he has the wish. He has his amulet with him, too."

The tomb raider rubbed her forehead. Alison was right, but James couldn't use the wish if he was dead and there were no guarantees how long his enemies would risk letting him live.

*Damn you, James.*

"How do you even know any of this?" Alison asked.

"That AET lieutenant, Maria Hall—the one who helped saved his ass last time—she gave me a call. I don't even know how the hell she has my number, but she explained the situation about how your dad is participating in basically the world's stupidest pay-per-view fight, and I called you to let you know."

"But not Dad? Shouldn't he be warned?"

"She's got someone else calling to warn him." Shay marched over to one of the pine trees and kicked the trunk several times. "I figured you deserved to know, and if I called him, nothing would happen but me screaming at him for ten minutes straight. That would feel good for me, but wouldn't be helpful."

Alison laughed. "Probably. After we're done here, I think I should be the one to call him, so at least somebody close is talking to him about this."

"Fine," Shay replied through gritted teeth. "I have a lot of aggression to work out before I speak with James Brownstone again."

"You do need to remember that he took care of himself before the two of us ever entered his life. He can be stubborn and make mistakes, but it's also not like he's a guy who doesn't know how to deal with danger."

Shay finished kicking the poor defenseless pine tree. "Fine. I'll just try to believe in him and his stupid amulet."

"That's all we can do. I know it'll be hard, but I'll be home soon, and then I can help keep him in check."

"You mean help me kill him?"

Alison laughed. "I don't think we should kill Dad. Promise me you won't."

"I won't," Shay grumbled.

22

James frowned as he put his truck into park and turned it off. The Salton Sea was just as he remembered it—nothing but sand, rocks, and dirt for miles. The water that had once been there had left its mark but was long gone.

*Where's Lars? If that fucker made me drive all the way out here just to flake out, I hope Tyler tells everyone how much of a chickenshit he is. Fuck, I'll have Heather spread that shit around.*

For all James knew Lars had teleported there. The bounty hunter still had a few hundred yards to hike to the actual coordinates. The battlefield was nestled between several small and large dunes, but James didn't want to drive his truck over there and risk even more injury to his old friend.

He glared at the crack in the windshield before opening his door and stepping outside. The harsh sun beat down on him.

"Yeah, I was a dumbass to pick this place again," James

muttered. "But I might as well get ready. I've got some ass to kick."

He reached under his shirt and yanked the metal separator off the back of his amulet. The alien artifact burned as it touched his chest. The whispers erupted immediately in his mind.

*Initiation.*

There'd been a brief second of understanding followed by a feeling of anticipation, but the word had been clear this time. Alien, but understandable.

*Initiation? What the fuck does that mean?*

Pain blossomed from the point of contract, knocking the question of James' head. The agony spread to the rest of his chest, then to his head and limbs.

James hissed at the fire burning through every cell in his body. The whispers returned, quiet and insistent. The amulet was ready for battle.

He took several deep breaths and threw open the back of the truck to grab his equipment, including his potions, grenades, and knives. Lars was a level five, so James wasn't about to make the mistake of underestimating him.

James' phone rang on the console, and he pulled it out. Tyler.

*Better not fucking chew me out again about being out of town, asshole.*

"What?" James rumbled into the phone. "I'm trying to get ready here."

*Guess it's a good thing I finally bothered to get a phone with backup satellite service.*

He thought about asking Heather to provide backup, but Tyler was already watching the area, and this was supposed to be a one-on-one confrontation. If it went well, even if Lars was taken down, it might be a trick they could use on a few other high-level bounties.

"I've got active camera feeds," Tyler began. "Also got some drones flying around with good vision." He sighed. "But there's a problem. A big fucking problem, and you need to know about it before you hit the site."

James cradled the phone with his neck as he slipped on his tactical harness. "What? I don't see any other cars or trucks here. Did that fucker run?"

"No, kind of the opposite, and that's the problem."

"What do you mean?" James finished putting on the harness and loading magazines into it.

"Lars double-crossed us. He's got at least two other guys with him, two level fours. One's a wizard and the other's some sort of gun mage, from what I've found out. That's three badasses coming at you at once." Tyler let out another long sigh. "You've got to believe me, Brownstone. I didn't plan this shit. I would have called you sooner, but Lars had two goons watching me and they had my phone. You can ask Lieutenant Hall later about the beat-down they gave me. I risked my handsome face for you."

James grunted. "I don't think you would plan something like this. You're a dick, but you're not a psychopath."

Tyler chuckled. "You should also know that Maria is pissed at both of us. She chewed my ass out enough for the both of us, but if you make it through this, you might want to avoid her for a while. I think she might try to put her foot up your ass."

James stopped loading magazines into his harness. "Shit, Lieutenant Hall knows about all this?"

"Yeah. Other than her being pissed, what's the big deal?"

"She might…tell some people I know, is all, and they'll be pissed."

"Some people you know?" Tyler laughed. "You sound like you're afraid of a woman finding out. You got a girlfriend, Brownstone? How did you hide that shit from me?"

"Fuck off, Tyler. None of your fucking business." James grabbed a few grenades and clipped them onto his tactical belt.

"Hey, don't worry about it. Anyway, I still have faith in your ability to kick ass. I've never lost money betting on you, and…fuck. Sonofabitch." Scratching filled the other end of the line.

"What's going on?"

Tyler muttered something before coming back over the line. "Someone just took out all my drones. Fuckers. I had eyes on Lars and Patrick—that's the wizard—but I don't have eyes on the third guy—the gun mage. Lars and Patrick are behind a large dune about a hundred yards out from the coordinates."

James started slipping throwing knives into sheaths. "At least now I know the fuckers are already here."

"Without the drones, I'm not going to have a lot of the good aerial camera angles. And that's if they don't jam the shit."

"So sorry. Next time, make sure you don't get double-crossed by a cop-killing psychopath." James grunted and slid a K-Bar into his final open sheath. "You're still gonna make a shitload off the betting, even if they take out every camera."

"Okay, okay. I'm sorry. Look, like I said, I still believe in you, asshole. I haven't lost money yet by betting on you, and I'm betting heavily. So if you die, it won't just be hard on you. It'll be hard on me."

James snorted. "Love your priorities. Doesn't matter. Let's make lots of money. I've got to save up for Disneyland."

"That isn't too far off. No matter how much money you make, there is a way to spend it all there. They make Happy Magic Land seem cheap by comparison."

Both men laughed.

"See you, Tyler." James ended the call and lowered his phone.

He was about to stick it in his pocket when it rang again. He lifted it back to his face.

"What, Tyler?"

Alison laughed. "It's not Tyler."

James' stomach tightened. The timing of her call was too perfect.

"What's up, kid?"

"Tell me you've got the amulet with you. Please tell me that you've already got it on."

The amulet whispered in his mind. Pride, maybe.

James sighed. "Yeah, but how did you know I needed it?"

A few beats of silence ticked by. "That's not important. What *is* important is that Mom is going to rip your manhood off if you get hurt doing your stupid pay-per-view event. She's pretty hot right now since she's worried."

James frowned. "What? Okay, I don't know how you know about this. Well, I have an idea, but I guess that's not important. Why would Shay be that mad about it? I'm a bounty hunter. I go after bad guys. The only difference this time is that I knew where they'd be, so why I am in trouble?"

"Are you serious right now?"

He shrugged. "I'm just saying. Maybe things haven't gone the way I planned, but that isn't different from any other bounty, so why would she be so worried?"

"You know how you can tell if someone's lying to themselves?"

James closed the back door of his truck. He had all the equipment he needed. "You look at their soul energy?"

"No, Dad. That's how I would know." She laughed. "I meant, how do *you* know if you're lying to yourself?"

He leaned against the side of his truck. "I don't lie to myself. Ever."

"Everyone does, and I know *you* did, but given what Mom was saying, it's obvious that you didn't tell her. Are you going to honestly tell me you didn't know about this pay-per-view thing for the last few days? It doesn't sound like something that'd be set up in a day."

James winced. "Yeah, I've known about it for a few days."

"Which means you didn't tell her on purpose, so you're lying to yourself if you're saying that you didn't purposely keep it from her. That means that, on some level, you knew she'd worry."

James groaned and scrubbed a hand over his face. "Well, I didn't want to distract her. She needs to concentrate on… Okay, you're right. I'm sorry. I'll tell her that next time I talk to her."

"I'm glad you understand. Now get out there and kick

their butts, and maybe wear a cup next time Mom's home. And you owe me a show when I get home, too."

"Sure. Maybe we can go see Hamilton at the Pantages." James smiled.

"Love you, Dad."

"Love you too, Alison." He hung up and pocketed his phone.

*So even if I survive Lars and his asshole friends, I still have to survive Shay.*

---

James marched toward the coordinates, thinking about everything Alison had said. She was right. He could have told Shay, but he'd held back.

*Fuck. That's not the way to have a relationship. She's got every right to be pissed at me when she comes back.*

As James approached the appointed area, he frowned. Still no sign of Lars or anyone else. He wasn't that worried about taking on more than one at a time, but he needed them to at least be somewhere he could see them.

He looked at the far dunes. Tyler had said they were there, but they might have moved.

James considered calling Heather, but it wouldn't help. Even if she could get drones in the area, they'd just be taken out like Tyler's.

It was time to apply the same strategy everyone was always trying to apply to him.

"Fucking Lars," James shouted. "Why don't you come out and face me? I thought you were ready to face me, but you're just a pussy, huh? A fake reputation."

Something slammed into James' chest. Pain spiked through his ribs, and he fell to the ground, blood soaking into his shirt.

The amulet shouted in his mind, furious.

"You're telling me," he muttered. He hissed and scrambled back to his feet, running zigzag toward a nearby dune and trying to ignore the pain. Something else whizzed by his head. Someone was blasting at him with high-powered, high-velocity rounds that could wound him but not make any noise.

*Fucking gun mage.*

Bullet after bullet struck behind him, kicking up dust and rock. A bullet grazed his thigh, and another clipped his shoulder.

James grunted and continued running toward the dune. He leapt behind an extensive outcropping, trying to ignore the pain from his wounds. The throbbing in his leg made him wonder if the bone had been damaged.

"That shit got past you, huh? That means someone with a big-ass gun is out there. If I didn't have you, I'd probably have a hole the size of Kansas in me."

The amulet raged in his mind. Vengeance. Anger.

The bounty hunter ignored his angry body partner for a moment and grabbed one of the healing potions from a pouch. "Glad I got a six-pack from Zoe."

He downed the potion, and his wounds sealed themselves in under fifteen seconds.

James eyed the empty potion bottle. "Guess the tweaked recipe was a good thing after all."

The amulet continued murmuring loudly in his mind.

*Kill.*

James blinked. The word might be alien in his mind, but the translation rang perfectly in his thoughts.

"I'd love to kill the asshole, but he's a sniper and I've got no eyes on him. Unless you have some brilliant ideas, shut the fuck up. I'm guessing the gun mage can make his gun super-quiet, so I don't have a prayer of figuring out where he's shooting from. I don't know how much you can understand me now, but if you got any other tricks, it's time to fucking show them."

The amulet fell silent for a few seconds. Bullets pinged and sparked against the outcropping. The sniper hadn't given up. If James stood, he'd be picked off in a second.

*Increase.*

Pain shot through James' eyes, and he groaned and slumped over. There was fire shooting through his eyeballs.

"What…the…fuck?"

The pain abated, and the amulet shouted in his mind.

*Kill.*

James blinked. Faint green lines arced away from the rock toward a dune in the distance.

"What the…"

*Kill.*

James nodded slowly. "Showing me where he is? Yeah, I can do that then." He took a few deep breaths and turned his head, taking note of the lines leading to the dune. A decent distance, but if he moved hard and fast, he shouldn't take too many hits.

He pulled out his .45 and squeezed off several shots in the opposite direction. After emptying his clip, he reloaded and grabbed two frag grenades.

*Shit. Wish I'd packed some smoke grenades.*

"Okay, hopefully, our guy thinks I'm gonna go the wrong way. Time to fucking move." James tossed grenades to either side.

The bounty hunter burst into a sprint when the grenades exploded, shifting direction every few yards as he closed on the target dune. Bullets tore up the ground but didn't clip the speeding bounty hunter.

The green lines faded from his vision. He wasn't sure if it reflected a limitation of the amulet, or if it was just trying not to distract him.

James threw another grenade toward the back of the dune, and someone yelled from behind it. He took the opportunity to stop dodging and barrel straight toward the dune.

A dark form crested the hill, a huge rifle with glowing runes covering the barrel in hand. Blood trailed down the side of his face.

James didn't hesitate. He put three bullets into the sniper's chest and the man fell and rolled down the dune, leaving a trail of blood.

"One down."

23

James cracked his knuckles. He had a smile on his face, and tension drifted away from his body. He'd half-worried about the ambush, but he didn't have to read a lot of Sun Tzu to understand that if an ambush failed, it put the enemy force on the defensive.

*Fuckers got overconfident. Thought they could win, but they didn't know about my potions or my defenses.*

He snorted. The more James considered things, the more insulted he was. Lars'd thought he had the upper hand but had badly underestimated the bounty hunter.

Lars using a gun-mage sniper to win didn't impress James. Hell, the gun-mage assassin the Harriken had sent after him had been far more dangerous.

*Wait, is that the point? Is the fucker just testing me?*

James grunted. Overconfidence could get him killed, even with potions and his amulet.

*Kill,* the amulet whispered.

"Huh. Better than dying." James shook his head. "What's wrong, Lars?" he shouted. "That was your big ambush? Some fucking sniper behind a dune?" He gestured toward the dead man. "It stung a little, but otherwise big fucking deal. I've had tougher times taking down level threes than I had dealing with that asshole. If you want to kill me, you better come at me with everything you got. Otherwise, only one of us is leaving this place still moving."

Lars and Patrick stepped out from behind a dune. The level-five's skin was already gray and hard, like he'd been covered with a thin layer of rock. The wizard's bone wand dangled from his fingers, the feathers at the end blowing lightly in the warm summer breeze.

The bounty shrugged. "You know what they say, fucker. You never know until you try."

James snorted. "Did you honestly think that would work? You think no one's ever tried to shoot me before?"

"I think that Victor's killed a lot of fuckers before you." Lars smirked. "But you got me all wrong, Brownstone. Some of this is about seeing if this shit is a waste of my time. Some of this is just whittling you down, just to be sure."

Patrick stepped forward.

Lars shook his head. "Not yet."

"But we could finish his ass."

The other man's mouth contorted into a sneer. "Don't fucking take my entertainment from me, Patrick. This isn't just about killing Brownstone. I didn't drive three hours for a five-minute fucking fight, okay? I want my money's worth, fucker."

The wizard frowned and stepped back. "Okay, okay. Don't get your panties in a twist."

James looked at the two. "What are you playing at, Lars?"

"More fun. This shit is entertaining." The gray-skinned man glanced toward another dune.

Two more large men stepped out, identical twins who dwarfed James. The bounty hunter grunted. He recognized them as level-four bounties.

"The Winter brothers? I thought they were still hiding out in Mexico."

The twins smiled.

"We flew up when we heard about this shit," one explained.

The other nodded. "How could we pass up the chance to help beat down the famous James Brownstone?"

Lars laughed. "Yeah. You see, when your boy Tyler called me and started asking about fighting, it got me to thinking. I was thinking that I should kick your ass, but then I thought that what I *really* wanted was for you to be fucking humiliated before I took you down." He shook his head and shrugged. "So I reached out to a bunch of people, and we all agreed we'd take shots at you." He held up a finger. "But, you know, honor among thieves and fucking shit like that. So Victor wanted to do his thing, and the Winter brothers wanted to do their thing, too. I don't give a fuck as long as I get my money and time's worth."

James grunted. "What, so this is some sort of multi-stage shit?"

"Yeah, something like that, fucker." Lars pointed to Victor's body. "Victor was Round One. The Winters are Round Two. Me and my boy Patrick are Round Three."

"Sounds like you're afraid to just come after me."

Lars shook his head. "Nah, fucker. You of all people know how much people will pay for the great James Brownstone to die. Maybe assholes are too afraid to be open about it, but if you know where to look, you'll get a reward." He grinned. "I'm fine if you're dead, but it's even better if I can get money out of it. Even if I don't get the reward, I have a shitload of money bet with that bitch Tyler on your ass dying."

James snorted. "Too bad you won't live to collect on that bet."

"Whatever." Lars nodded to the twins and gestured toward James. "Fucking kill him already, or die. I don't give a shit which. Getting boring now."

The Winters brothers advanced, wearing identical frowns and smacking their fists into their palms.

James whipped out his .45 and fired a single round into each brother. They stumbled, but the wounds sealed a second later.

*Yeah. I guess level fours wouldn't go down that easily. Maybe I should start collecting a few magic knives or shit like Shay, or borrow her Masamune sword or something.*

The bounty hunter grunted. From what he'd read, the twins' mother had been a witch who'd used some sort of protection spell on them in the womb, even before the truth of magic became known. Regeneration and enhanced strength made for a hell of a combination.

James holstered his .45. "Nice trick." He'd just need to think of a good way to slow their regeneration while he finished both men off.

"Scared yet, Brownstone?" one of the twins asked.

"Have any last words?" the other wondered.

The bounty hunter took a few steps forward. "You seriously think you're gonna intimidate me with that sort of shit? Level fours I can beat without even bringing my A-game, so I'll give you this chance to turn around and fuck off before I beat you down." He pointed to Lars. "*His* ass is going down, though."

The twins glared at James, and a few seconds later they yelled in unison and rushed him.

*Nobody can say I didn't give these fuckers a chance to get away.*

James sprinted forward to meet their charge. He threw his shoulder into the first twin, sending him stumbling back with a grunt.

The other brother grabbed James' arm and yanked him back. He slammed his fist into James' face several times, the blows barely stinging thanks to the amulet. The twin picked up the bounty hunter and brought him hard down on his knee in an attempt to break his back.

James bounced off and landed on the ground. He rolled and hopped to his feet, rubbing his back. A little ache and probably a bruise, but nothing worse.

The bounty hunter shook his head. The amulet murmured away, a certain smugness radiating from its words. He still couldn't decode much other than 'kill.'

*Whatever your name is, if you have one, thanks. Without you, that first asshole probably would have taken me down.*

The twins jogged back a few yards and stood together, frowns on their faces.

The bounty hunter shot them a grin. "What's the matter, not used to people not snapping in half when you try hard? Sorry, assholes. Last time I was here, it took some pretty powerful magic to hurt me. I don't think you assholes have that. Just because you're tough doesn't mean you're gonna win against me."

"Fuck you, Brownstone," the men growled in unison.

James shook his head. "Is that shit supposed to be intimidating? It's funny, more than anything. Gonna get some rubber balls to bounce at the same time? Maybe wear the same pretty bow in your hair?" He raised his hand and gestured for them to come at him. "Let's finish this shit. I still have to kick Lars' and the wizard's asses."

The brothers took a few steps to either side, their eyes narrowed. James took the opportunity to hurl two sonic grenades. The whine filled the air and both men collapsed, clutching their ears. Apparently, unlike with his amulet, their sturdiness didn't protect them from that kind of attack.

*Didn't see that coming, did you, assholes?*

James rushed over to the first brother. He yanked him up and slammed his fist into his face several times. His head snapped back, and blood spurted out, but the wounds healed. After the tenth hit, the man moaned and his eyes fluttered closed.

*Guess regenerating doesn't save you from being knocked out.*

The bounty hunter tossed the man to the ground and planted his booted foot on the stomach of the other brother. He dropped knee-first, to the man's chest, and alternated pummeling him with both fists until blood covered the bounty hunter's shirt and harness.

James stood up. The second Winter brother was breathing but unconscious. His battered face had already begun knitting itself back together.

The bounty hunter shook out his hands. "I should use those sonic things more often. My girlfriend uses them a lot, but I've avoided them. I guess I just like to fucking waste people more directly or go old-school with a flash-bang." He shrugged at Lars. "All this high-tech shit can fail. I like to keep it simple."

Lars snorted. "Fuck off, Brownstone. I'm not impressed." He nodded to Patrick. "Fucking finish them off while they're out. Pussies."

"What?"

The level five narrowed his eyes at Patrick. "Or you can deal with me."

The redheaded wizard lifted his wand, and a massive fireball grew in front of it over several seconds. James leapt to the side as the blast crashed into the downed men.

The blast wave knocked him to the ground, and after a few seconds the stench of burnt flesh filled the air. Only the charred skeletons remained of the men.

*Fuck. Can't regenerate if you don't have a body.*

James stood and stared at Lars. "Don't you think some of your fellow criminals might have something to say about that?"

A sick grin appeared on Lars' face. "Nah. Not like we're in a union, fucker. I was hoping you'd kill them. It's entertaining, and if they aren't strong enough to take you out, who cares?" He cracked his knuckles. "But it's time for Round Three. I'm going to enjoy killing you, Brownstone. Going to enjoy seeing the panic in your eyes as I'm fucking you up and you understand, in those last few seconds, that you're going to die."

The bounty hunter reached for a sonic grenade, but he was out.

*Whatever. I'll beat their asses down the old-fashioned way, then.*

The amulet's quiet whispers became strident and understandable.

*Kill.*

James snorted. *Yeah, no argument there.*

---

The crowd in the Black Sun winced as the fireball exploded and incinerated the Winter brothers. Tyler had been alternating camera feeds on the big screen on his wall.

The information broker shook his head and clucked his tongue. Maria was right. This was the problem with these high-level assholes. They didn't have any respect for boundaries. Killing a guy because he came at you was one thing, but murdering him after he helped you, even if for his own reasons, was grade-A bullshit.

*I hope you tear this fucker's head off, Brownstone, and not just for the money.*

*Oh, yeah, the money. Almost forgot what this was about.*

Tyler rushed over to the odds board and slapped it with the back of his hand. He had no idea who'd come up with the idea of adding real time odds and in-fight betting, but it was a fucking gold mine.

"There you have it, folks," he yelled. "The odds have changed in Brownstone's favor with the defeat of the Winters brothers and Victor. They keep wounding him, but they aren't stopping him. The Bounty Hunter One-Man Army. The Scourge of Harriken. The Granite Ghost."

"That's bullshit," a man shouted. "He didn't kill those guys, Patrick did. That better not pay out anything."

Tyler tapped a box on the board. "Fair enough. All these deaths categories clearly state that Brownstone has to be the one killing people or be killed, so you're right, Patrick blowing people up doesn't count."

"That's right." The man crossed his arms and beamed a smug smile at the information broker.

"But Brownstone knocked them out." Tyler erased a few of the boxes and started filling in new numbers. "Which means he's not taking on as many people at once. The early Brownstone adopters are the ones who will really profit from this."

The angry biker from before reached into his wallet to yank out even more bills. "Fuck that. I'm gonna double-down on Lars. Just because Brownstone beat some small-fry pussies don't mean shit. Lars is a level five, and Brownstone won't be able to win against him." He pointed at Tyler but spoke to the crowd. "Don't you get it? This fucker is just trying to get us to cover his dumb bets for Brownstone. He's on Team Brownstone, and has been for a while."

Tyler rushed up to the man and got right in his face. "Don't you fucking dare. I'm a businessman. All I want to do is make money. I'll take any opportunity that presents itself, whether it involves Brownstone or anyone else. As long as that bounty hunter can make me money I'll bet on him or send bounties at him, but don't you ever say I'm fucking Team Brownstone. I fucking hate his ass."

*I do, don't I?*

The biker grunted and shoved Tyler away. "Whatever. I'll just take your money and make you cry that way, bitch."

The bar owner stomped back toward the table in front of the odds board. Kathy sat there, checking through the online bets on a laptop they'd brought from the office.

Tyler slid into a chair. "I'm *not* on Team Brownstone," he muttered.

*This isn't about anything but money. I only warned him because it's a reputation thing. It's not like I give a shit if he dies. People have to know that. If I liked Brownstone, I wouldn't have helped send a level-five psycho at him.*

Kathy snickered. "There are worse teams to be on. You're practically business partners with the guy, and you've been making eyes at a cop. Just something to think about."

Tyler's head shot in her direction. "What are you getting at?"

"Just saying, maybe you're less of a criminal mastermind than you think if you're buddying up to a bounty hunter and a cop." She shrugged. "Nothing to be ashamed of. Brownstone and Hall are better people to hang out with than psychos like Lars Hansen."

"Maria's the reason this place is neutral ground. What do you want me to do, tell her to piss off? I'm making a lot of money and have a lot more opportunities because it's neutral ground. And I don't leave money on the table."

Kathy rolled her eyes. "Keep telling yourself that, Tyler. Whatever. I'm just the employee. Ignore me, boss man."

*This is about money on the table. Nothing more. Nothing less.*

"I think they are about to go at it," a gang member in the corner shouted.

Tyler snapped his attention back to the screen. Patrick and Lars had spread out. The wizard had his wand up, and the level five was grinning at Brownstone like a hungry cat in front of a cornered mouse.

The information broker hopped up. "Get in your bets. It could last an hour, or it could be over in seconds. You don't want to wait until it's too late. You don't want to lay awake tonight asking yourself, 'Could have I made a big score off James Brownstone?'"

Several men grabbed their phones to make electronic transfers. Others grabbed their wallets.

Tyler smirked.

*Team Brownstone. I'm not on fucking Team Brownstone. I'm on Team Greenback.*

Lars kept circling James with a stupid grin plastered on his face. "You could just get on your knees and let me beat your ass, Brownstone. If you do, maybe I'll make it quick. Otherwise, it's going to be long and really, *really* hurt. Because I really want to see you cry and beg."

*Fuck, this guy likes to talk. He's almost King Pyro-bad.*

Patrick offered no verbal taunts, but his raised wand was more than enough threat as he circled the opposite direction.

*The other guy's too focused. That could be a problem.*

James' gaze flicked between the men. Lars was the greater threat, but the bounty hunter wasn't sure if he could take a direct hit from the wizard's fireball after what he'd just witnessed.

*Need that fucker to clip me so you can adapt.*

The amulet's response was straightforward. *Kill.*

*Yeah, thought you'd say that.*

James grunted and kept his distance from both men. "You're not leaving here, Lars. I might not kill you, but I'm gonna at least break your legs. Then I'll call AET and have them pick you up. I'm sure the cops would love to send your ass to an ultra-max for what you did in Atlanta."

"Fuck you, Brownstone. And fuck the cops. I'm not afraid of you, and I'm not afraid of them."

The bounty hunter ducked as Patrick's wand spat out a quick firebolt. The heat warmed his face as the solid orange-red bolt flew inches over his head.

*Damn. Don't want to take one in the face yet. Or ever.*

The amulet murmured excitedly.

James ignored his partner and fired several rounds toward Patrick. The bullets bounced off and landed on the ground as molten pools.

He sprinted toward the men as Patrick continued launching firebolts. A bolt struck James in the leg and he hissed, collapsing to one knee. He tried to ignore the agony of the deep burn as he pushed himself back to his feet, the amulet murmuring and obviously excited about a new kind of attack.

Lars laughed. "That's all you got, Brownstone? I might not even need to get involved. And here I thought I was going to have to double-team you. What a fucking disappointment. Maybe your rep is all talk."

James fired several times at Lars, but the bullets bounced off his hardened gray skin with a spark. He holstered his weapon. This wasn't a fight he was going to win with a gun.

*Wonder where I can get a magic gun? Do I have to be a wizard to use one?*

Ignoring the searing pain in his leg, the bounty hunter stalked toward Patrick.

*Maybe because I can talk to you now, I trust you more. Or maybe it's because I know how you work. Let's show this fucker how we do things.*

Patrick snorted. "See you in Hell, Brownstone." Another firebolt blasted into James' chest.

The intense heat burned a hole in his shirt, but rather than the searing agony he felt in his leg only a brief burning sensation passed over his skin.

The wizard blinked. "What the fuck?"

James continued advancing. "Surprised, asshole?"

---

A loud "Oooooh" rose from the crowd in the Black Sun when James absorbed the blast.

Tyler stared at the screen, surprised despite having bet on the bounty hunter. "Does he have some sort of anti-magic artifact?" He turned to Kathy and opened his mouth, but closed it when the doubtful biker from before rushed over.

"I need to place some bets on Brownstone," the biker announced. He looked at the TV with panic in his eyes. "Now. I want to pull my earlier bets."

Tyler shook his head. "That's not how this shit works, and you know it. Don't place bets you don't believe in.'

"But I don't have any more cash on me. Come on, man."

The information broker tapped his phone on the table. "Got a bank account? Let's do some electronic transfers. You can still hedge and earn some sweet Brownstone cash. I'm equipped to handle that."

"Oh, yeah. Let's do that."

Patrick blasted Brownstone a few more times in his arms and legs. The wizard was doing a good job of destroying the bounty hunter's clothes, but his attacks were now only leaving red spots with some minor surface burns rather than the deep tissue burn in Brownstone's leg from the first attack.

His hands shaking, the biker fished out his phone and began furiously tapping to try to initiate a money transfer. "Come on. Come on."

Tyler allowed himself to grin.

*See, asshole? Betting against Brownstone is like betting against the sun coming up. I told you assholes before, but you didn't listen.*

Lars grunted. "What the fuck, Patrick? Kill the motherfucker."

"I'm trying." The wizard backpedaled. "I need a few seconds to generate a bigger attack. Keep him off me. I don't get it. He should already be dead."

"For fuck's sake! Fine, I'll fucking kill him myself. Wanted to anyway." Lars let out a low growl and charged James.

*Here it comes.*

If the bounty hunter hadn't had an injured leg, he might have been able to dodge. Instead, the literally hardened criminal slammed into James, his armored rocky skin turning him into a solid battering ram.

James grunted and stumbled back only a few feet. The pain in his leg was a lot worse than what he felt from the collision.

Something approaching surprise crossed Lars' face. He'd obviously expected the bounty hunter to go flying.

*Simple kinetic force doesn't work much anymore, asshole. My amulet had that shit handled a long time ago.*

James took the opportunity presented by the other man's surprise to reach down and grab a healing potion. The first bottle he pulled up was already broken in half. He tossed it to the ground and grabbed the second, downing the contents just before Lars slammed into him again, this time knocking him down.

He rolled to his side, the pain in his leg lessening, and the wound sealing itself. Lars slammed an armored foot into James, launching him several feet this time, but it became clear a couple seconds later that the real point of the attack was providing a better target for the wizard.

James managed to duck, his shoulder and side taking a glancing blow from the white-hot flame. The ball exploded in front of him, knocking him down. He hissed at the mild burns now covering his body, and a few vanished from the lingering effects of the healing potion.

Patrick blinked and shook his head. "How is he still alive? This is fucking unbelievable."

"Sorry to disappoint you, asshole," James rumbled, and stood.

Lars laughed and clapped. "Now *this* is what I'm talking about. This is actually fun, and here I thought you'd die pretty quickly. Thanks for not making this shit boring as fuck, Brownstone."

James snorted. "Oh, this isn't the part where you go on

about how my rep is all smoke and mirrors? Maybe you're not a total fucking moron, then."

"Nah, fucker. I believe your rep. Why do you think I brought all my friends? You're worth it, Brownstone. Just figured it wouldn't hurt to soften you up. Winning a fight is as much about strategy as strength."

"So you *are* afraid. Thought so."

Lars shrugged. "Sometimes it's about just using your noggin, fucker. You're a thug, so maybe you don't get that. At the end of the day, you need to live to fight another day."

James grunted. "You think that's clever?"

"Doesn't matter if *you* don't. You'll be fucking dead soon."

Patrick shook his head. "There's no way you should have been able to survive those hits." He lifted his wand again, his arm shaking. "No way." He took a deep breath. "You won't survive next time. You're dead, Brownstone."

James charged the wizard. A firebolt missed his shoulder by a hairsbreadth. The bounty hunter yanked his K-Bar from its scorched sheath.

"A knife?" The wizard sneered. "You'll never get that to my body, Bro—"

Patrick was right. James didn't get it to his body. Instead, he sliced the man's wand in half with a stroke.

The bounty hunter didn't get a chance for a follow-up attack since Lars grabbed him and threw him in the opposite direction. James thudded into the ground and rolled several feet before hopping back up. His K-Bar was embedded in the dirt and sand.

*Kill,* the amulet whispered.

*I'm working on it, asshole. Without the wand, that wizard's nothing.*

Patrick was staring at his sliced wand, disbelief etched into his face. Lars snickered and backhanded the man to the ground. A sickening crunch sounded as his head hit the ground and his neck snapped.

James shook his head. "You're one sick asshole, and I've run into a lot of them."

Lars shrugged. "What can I say, fucker? I've got to be me, and I don't have time for weak-ass pussies who can't do much. He had his shot, and he couldn't finish you. Don't worry. You're joining him soon."

The two men started circling one another.

"You think you can take me after everything you've seen?" James asked. "You're not just a sick asshole, you're an arrogant prick."

"We'll see who the arrogant prick is. I think you're fucking dead in the next few minutes, Brownstone."

———

Shay stared at the images of the fight on her phone, her jaw tight. Peyton had accessed the Black Sun's systems and was streaming Tyler's camera feeds directly to her.

*Damn it, James!*

Her lover had been doing well so far, but he'd also only been facing weaker opponents. The psycho Lars Hansen didn't seem even remotely concerned that the bounty hunter had gone through so many of his little helpers. Fortunately, with the help of the healing potion, James was as good as when he started the fight.

*This is why you don't agree to dumbass stunts like this, idiot.*

The tomb raider delivered another few satisfying kicks to a nearby tree trunk. The pounding heart was familiar, but she wasn't used to complete helplessness.

Shay let out a long sigh.

*I guess I shouldn't be so upset. It's not like he's doing anything different than when I first met him. He's opened up to me, but that doesn't mean he's changed from being a bounty hunter who goes after nasty assholes.*

*Sure, I've changed. I'm not the same cold-blooded killer I once was, but when we went down to Mexico together, he took a detour to go after a necromancer the Mexican military was trying to bomb into submission. He makes this guy look like a Boy Scout in comparison.*

Shay groaned. Oh, they spent time together and chatted, but some of her most exciting memories with James involved them killing dozens if not hundreds of people together. Harriken, magical assassins, the Nuevo Gulf Cartel. Hard to complain about him getting into danger when she enjoyed getting into danger with him.

*I just wish I could be there with you.*

The tomb raider routinely went on jobs that were, in many ways, more dangerous than the bounties James dealt with, given the strange monsters and magical beings she encountered. She didn't let him know many of the details, but there was some thick hypocrisy accompanying her complaining about him going after a level-five bounty when she'd had to flee invisible armies and had fought a demon-possessed elf who might have been planning to invade another planet.

She leaned her back against the tree trunk she'd been

kicking and slumped until her knees were at her chest. "The dumbass is just learning what a relationship is like and how to deal with a kid. Maybe I'm asking too much. Stupid fucking men, being stupid all the damned time. How our species continues to exist is a wonder no one may ever understand."

The tomb raider smiled when James slashed the wand in half.

*Yeah, I have to remember that you are James Brownstone.*

"Nice move. It won't always work for you, but it's a good tactic. Now it's really just you and Lars."

Shay nodded to herself. She'd have to remember to compliment him on it once the fight was over. She needed to let him know she respected him.

James would survive. He *had* to survive, and he had the Whispering Amulet of Doom, which had already proven how quickly it could adapt. She'd personally tested it.

*Wonder if any of the other dumbasses watching this understand what they are witnessing, and now know why they should never, ever fuck with him.*

Most of James' lower shirt was in burnt tatters, but the upper part still concealed his amulet and provided a nice view of the abs that proved her lover should be crowned Emperor of Abtopia.

*Don't die. I'll miss those.*

Shay blew out a breath. She shouldn't have called Alison in a fury. She might not be prepared to let the girl call her Mom, but she was still Aunt Shay, so she needed to be strong and act like a damned adult.

The tomb raider ran a hand through her hair. "I guess this is the hard part of love: worry."

Shay tapped out a quick text to Alison.

**Sorry I got so heated earlier. I appreciate you talking me down and contacting him. It was a good thing I didn't yell at him right before a fight. Wouldn't want him off his game.**

**No problem**, Alison replied. **I know we both love and worry about him.**

Shay returned her attention to the camera feed. "Just finish Lars off already, James."

---

James slammed a fist into Lars' face. He might as well have been hitting a rock wall. The bounty hunter shook out his fist, and the criminal knocked James back with a powerful blow.

An exchange of fierce punches followed, both men landing solid blows but both unable to do much damage.

*Kill,* the amulet hissed.

James tried a kick next, but it only sent Lars stumbling back a few feet.

*How do I finish this asshole off? Any ideas?*

*Enemy.*

*Yeah. Thanks for that.*

The bounty hunter backed up and narrowed his eyes. Every defense had a weakness. He just needed to find it.

Lars swaggered forward, grinning. "I'll give you credit, Brownstone. Those hits would have caved in most men's faces, but you're still standing; just a little burned and bloody. I guess we're similar. That's making this shit exciting."

"Nope, not similar at all. You're a psycho asshole. I'm a little OCD, at most."

"Psycho asshole? No, I'm just a realist, Brownstone." Lars took a few more steps toward James. "My question is, how long can you last?" He pointed at James. "You may be taking a lot of hits, but you're still hurt, and it's time to make sure that you stay hurt." He charged.

James brought up his fists but Lars ducked low, tackling him. The criminal threw a few stinging punches before the bounty hunter kicked him off and got back to his feet.

Lars laughed. "I win now."

"What the fuck are you talking about? That barely hurt."

The gray-skinned criminal pointed at the James' tactical belt. "Sorry, had to crush your little potions."

James kept his gaze focused on Lars while he felt in the pouch; nothing but glass shards and loose liquid.

"Fucker. Do you have any idea how expensive that shit was?'

"Don't worry, you'll be dead soon enough." Lars offered James a wide smile.

That was when the bounty hunter noticed a key detail: blood on the man's teeth.

James yanked out his .45, grateful it hadn't been incinerated in the blast. "Time to end this, you fucking psycho. Just so you know, I'm earning a shitload of money off my bets on this."

"A gun?" Lars stalked toward James. "You already tried that. Desperate, Brownstone?"

"Nope. Just tired of your ass and your mouth."

Lars took another step forward. "Then lay down and prepare to—"

Wisps of smoke floated off the edge of James' fired .45 as the bullet passed through Lars' open mouth, into his brain, and out of his head, along with a good chunk of bone.

James holstered his pistol as Lars' body fell backward, the criminal's gaze locked in a death stare.

"Learned that little trick in Japan. Say hi to the Devil for me, asshole."

25

A few days later, James leaned against a wall of the Brownstone Building watching the men go through PT led by Staff Sergeant Royce. The former gang members had always been strong, but it'd been interesting to watch their bodies slowly be sculpted into warrior physiques.

Crunches followed push-ups, which led to burpees.

Royce had kept on about strong minds and strong bodies. Given how the men had been performing in both LA and Las Vegas, James was a believer. He might not be a good leader or trainer, but at least he was good at delegating to men who were.

The Brownstone Agency had a bright future. It wasn't just about improving the lives of some ex-gang members. Once they finished getting all the men up to speed, they'd have to look into recruiting more trainees.

James ran his hand over the amulet underneath his shirt. He wasn't bonded with it, but the last couple of weeks had changed his perspective on the artifact. He could communicate with the thing, at least a little, and it had more potential than he'd realized.

*Huh. Shay said it probably had more powers I could unlock, but I didn't figure it'd happen that way.*

He still wasn't sure how much to trust the thing or what motivated it, but for now he'd keep it near him as he continued to delve into its secrets.

*Wonder what else the bad boy can do?*

James frowned. Relying on a self-aware alien amulet wasn't exactly high on the list of simple ways to live and work, but at the same time, he couldn't ignore such a useful tool. The amulet wasn't just an artifact. He'd been found with it, as if it were meant for him. A legacy of his parents perhaps, and his world.

The bounty hunter blew out a breath and shook his head. So many things had changed. He had been just a simple man who loved barbeque and lived alone with his dog.

Trey stepped out of the building in his workout shorts and T-shirt. He had a smile on his face "You know why I like you, James?"

James looked Trey's way. "Why? I was just standing here."

"Nah, you don't get it. It's because no matter what stupid shit I think I've done, you do stupider shit. It makes me feel better about my shit." Trey grinned. "But you keep surviving it. That shit with Lars and his motherfuckers is all over the internet now, you know. They're calling it the Brownstone Summer Beat-Down. Those motherfuckers never saw what was coming." He snorted. "They actually thought they were gonna win against James motherfucking Brownstone with that weak-ass attempt."

"Everyone thinks they can take me down. Some come closer than others, and someday some asshole might get lucky. You never know." James shrugged.

The door opened again, revealing Charlyce.

"I'm gonna shut everything down in the office and head to the orphanage now."

James nodded at her. "Thanks for all your help there."

"Says the man who donates so much money."

"Donating money is easy. Donating time is hard."

Charlyce offered her boss and nephew a final smile before slipping back into the building.

"All right, maggots," Royce shouted. "Now we're going to do some laps around the neighborhood. Stretch, and I'll be right back."

The drill instructor jogged over and picked up a brown paper bag from the ground and headed over to James.

He held out the bag. "I swear by this product, James."

James hoped so. It'd be critical to protecting a vital organ in a dangerous confrontation down the road.

The bounty hunter took the bag. "Thanks, Royce."

The drill instructor nodded and headed toward the street. The other men stopped stretching and hurried after him.

Trey nodded to James. "I better join them for that, at least. Paperwork's not a good excuse for missing PT." He jogged after the Marine and his boys.

James was just about to head inside the building when a police cruiser rolled into the parking lot. He frowned and walked toward it, only to relax when Sergeant Mack stepped out of the vehicle.

The cop laughed. "Yeah, I saw that look on your face, Brownstone. Sorry for showing up in the car all of a sudden. Took care of some stuff downtown, and thought I'd stop by before I headed back to the station."

James grunted. "No problem. What's up?"

"Figured I'd let you know I've got everything set up for our wood. We can start prepping tomorrow if you want."

"Good to hear. I think it'll be good to get the men all working on some quality barbeque. All this warrior philosophy and exercise shit is fine, but people need to know how to appreciate quality meat and do shit that doesn't involve kicking people's asses."

Mack smiled. "Yeah, I agree." His smile disappeared. "But that's not the only reason I stopped by." He rubbed the back of his neck.

*Fuck. That doesn't sound good.*

"What's the other reason?"

"Also wanted to let you know not to pull a stunt at the Salton Sea again like you just did. At least not anytime remotely soon."

"It turned out all right, didn't it?" James shrugged. "What's the big deal?"

Mack glanced at the police car and back at James. "You've got to understand… Lieutenant Hall is *pissed*. AET collected all those bodies when they arrived, but she's been bitching about it for days. About you being stupid and stubborn, and how you should have been working with AET and not doing video. All sorts of stuff. Don't give her another reason to notice you, Brownstone."

"So things are back to the way they used to be? She gunning for me?" James grunted. An angry AET lieutenant was the last thing he needed.

Mack shook his head. "Not saying that. Just saying don't piss her off again anytime soon."

"I wasn't trying to. I thought I was doing things the safe way."

"Only you could think that marching to a dried-up former inland sea to fight a level-five psycho is doing things the safe way." Mack laughed.

"Yeah, but—" James' phone chimed. "One second. Just need to check my texts. Shay's barely been talking to me the last few days. Think she's still pissed about what happened."

"You better apologize right away when you see her. Women want apologies."

The text wasn't from Shay but from Tyler. He wanted Brownstone to come over and discuss his winnings.

James looked up from his phone. "Sorry, but I've got something to take care of. Need to chat with Tyler at the Black Sun."

Mack stared at James. "Yeah. It's still weird for you to be going there on purpose and peacefully."

"Tyler's not so bad for a money-obsessed piece of shit." James shrugged. "Talk to you later, Mack."

"Talk to you later, Brownstone."

James made himself comfortable in the chair across from Tyler's desk as the information broker and temporary bookie stared at a spreadsheet on his computer. Royce's brown paper bag sat on the bounty hunter's lap.

"Damn," Tyler muttered.

"What?"

Tyler looked up from his computer. "Just thinking about how much money we made. Those idiots poured so much fucking money into Lars that I almost feel bad for them." The bar owner chuckled. "*Almost*. But the money makes that feeling go away."

"This probably won't work again, you know."

The information broker sighed. "Yeah, I know. Your beat-down was too good, and it was hard enough to find someone this time. Just keep an open mind. You never know what opportunities might present themselves."

"I don't know. My girlfriend's pretty pissed at me." James shrugged. "Not sure it's worth the trouble."

"Yeah, Maria came by to scream at me again for this. I still think it's not a big deal. All we did was add a little extra to what you do anyway. Everyone's freaking out for no good reason."

James grunted. "Yeah. Everything worked out exactly like we thought in the end, so what is the problem? It didn't end up being that different than a few bounties strung together."

"I agree, but chicks…what are you going to do?" Tyler sighed. "They aren't rational like guys."

"I've got one idea about what to do." James reached into the bag and pulled out a jock strap. He tossed it on the desk.

The other man eyed the accessory, his brow furrowed.

"What the fuck, Brownstone? You trying out for a football team?"

"Nope. You owe me one." James stood. "My daughter suggested I use this the next time I encountered my girlfriend. I figured you might need one the next time you saw Lieutenant Hall. That, and a bulletproof vest."

James took a deep breath as the garage door closed behind his F-350 and killed the engine. His doom wasn't that many feet away.

Thanks to his phone alerts he knew that Shay had come home early and was already in his house. He hadn't been looking forward to this, but he knew it was inescapable.

*Maybe I should bond with the amulet to be safe.*

The bounty hunter chuckled and stepped out of the truck. No use trying to run away from his destiny. He opened the side door and stepped into his home.

Shay stood in the living room, her arms crossed, frowning. "I've been waiting for you."

"Yeah, I figured." James cleared his throat. "Hey, Shay. Didn't know you were coming home early. You didn't text me to say you were."

"Figured I better show up before you went and did some other dumbass stunt." She snorted.

"You know, I was talking with Tyler earlier about that, and we both kind of were thinking about how it ended how we wanted. So is it really a big deal when you think about it?"

Shay's jaw dropped. "Yes, dumbass, it is a big deal when

you basically set yourself up to be ambushed. You got lucky these guys didn't have some weird-ass artifact that could have taken your head off. I'm sure the Whispering Amulet of Doom can't do much if you're dead."

James pondered that. He wasn't honestly sure, but he wasn't eager to test the theory. He opened his mouth to respond when Mack's earlier words replayed in his head.

*Women want apologies.*

*Oh, yeah, that makes sense.*

The bounty hunter shrugged. "I'm sorry."

Shay shook a finger at him. "Of course, you think… Wait, *what?*"

James nodded. "I'm sorry. I shouldn't have done it. I guess it ended okay, but it was crap, and I know it. Alison even pointed out how I didn't tell you, so that proves something. I wanted to take down some assholes and make some money, but I never wanted to piss you off or worry you or Alison."

Her face pinched, and her mouth twitched. James suspected she'd had a far-longer rant built up and didn't know what to do since he'd already surrendered.

*Thanks, Mack. I'll have to thank you later.*

"Well, don't do it again," Shay muttered, "or you'll bring the old Shay back. You want to go after bounties, do it the smart way, not some grandstanding gambling way involving that asshole Tyler. You can't trust that piece of shit."

"Okay. Fair enough."

She narrowed her eyes. Her face was still red, and there was something calculating in her eyes. "No, I can't let this go that easily. You made me feel helpless and pissed me off, and I need to take my revenge. I have to let out this aggression. Kicking trees didn't do enough."

"Your revenge? Kicking trees? What are you talking about?"

Shay stalked toward James, the corners of her mouth turning down. "This is how it feels, dumbass." She slammed her foot into his crotch and her eyes widened. "Dammit, who the hell told you to wear a cup?"

*FINIS*

THANK you for not only reading this story (or rather ALL of them) but also reading these author notes.

The tale of Mr. Brownstone is over...*But is also starting fresh in book 09.*

This is the last book where Brownstone is legally ... Wait...wait... I can't say the next thing, cause it gives away the next book.

*DAMN!*

Well...shit. What am I supposed to chat about now? How about how enemies become frenemies and perhaps... *based on shared pain...* reluctant acquaintances?

The opening of Book 09 is one whole chapter on something I personally find both interesting and full of opportunity to explore. I'm not giving away the whole premise, but lets just say that I use it as a way to show that shared confusion unites.

Right now, I'm sitting in a small Chinese restaurant in Las Vegas called the Great Wall of China. (It even has a large cardboard display of red brick wall... Not that one uses this type of break in the Great Wall but I digress.) I've eaten MAYBE half of the Beef Fried rice and about 16 oz of Coke and I'm freaking stuffed. With this many carbs, I'm not sure I'm going to be able to make it to my car before I fall asleep.

*Why do I do this to myself?*

Just a small hint about book 09, Alison is coming back to LA – she is on summer vacation and she learns that James believes she needs to learn a few new skills.

The Drow Queen makes a comeback, and James will have a few words for her.

People are going to try to take away his daughter, and he will be *damned* if that happens without a (few) fights.

Looking forward to the challenge James Brownstone wasn't prepared for…

*Women.*

Ad Aeternitatem,

Michael Anderle

**The Soul Stone Mage Series**

*** Sarah Noffke and Martha Carr ***

House of Enchanted (1) - The Dark Forest (2) - Mountain of Truth (3) - Land of Terran (4) - New Egypt (5) - Lancothy (6) - Virgo (7)

**The Kacy Chronicles**

*** A.L. Knorr and Martha Carr ***

Descendant (1) - Ascendant (2) - Combatant (3) - Transcendent (4)

**The Midwest Magic Chronicles**

*** Flint Maxwell and Martha Carr***

The Midwest Witch (1) - The Midwest Wanderer (2) - The Midwest Whisperer (3) - The Midwest War (4)

**The Fairhaven Chronicles**

*** with S.M. Boyce ***

Glow (1) - Shimmer (2) - Ember (3) - Nightfall (4)

# CONNECT WITH MICHAEL ANDERLE

**Michael Anderle Social**
**Website:**
**http://kurtherianbooks.com/**

**Email List:**
**http://kurtherianbooks.com/email-list/**

**Facebook Here:**
https://www.facebook.com/OriceranUniverse/
https://www.
facebook.com/TheKurtherianGambitBooks/

9 781642 022193